Great Adventure Stories

Two British adventurers strike out for a remote area of India in Rudyard Kipling's world-famous "The Man Who Would Be King."

In Anthony Hope's "The Sin of the Bishop of Modenstein," a young man of the cloth is the only person brave enough to try to rescue a kidnapped princess.

A brave cavalry officer secretly crosses enemy lines in "How the Brigadier Saved an Army," by Arthur Conan Doyle.

These and other dramatic stories explore the qualities of courage and heroism in this special collection of *Great Adventure Stories*.

Great Adventure Stories

Great Adventure Stories

A WATERMILL CLASSIC

Contents of this edition copyright © Troll Communications L.L.C. Watermill Press is an imprint and registered trademark of Troll Communications L.L.C.

Printed in the United States of America.

ISBN 0-8167-0801-0

10 9 8 7 6 5 4

Contents

Contents

Great Adventure Stories

Rudyard Kipling

The Man Who Would Be King

"Brother to a prince and fellow to a beggar if he be found worthy."

The law, as quoted, lays down a fair conduct of life, and one not easy to follow. I have been fellow to a beggar again and again under circumstances which prevented either of us finding out whether the other was worthy. I have still to be brother to a prince, though I once came near to kinship with what might have been a veritable king and was promised the reversion of a kingdom—army, law courts, revenue and police all complete. But, today, I greatly fear that my king is dead, and if I want a crown I must go and hunt it for myself.

The beginning of everything was in a railway train upon the road to Mhow from Ajmir. There had been a deficit in the budget, which necessitated traveling, not second class, which is only half as dear as first class, but by intermediate, which is very awful indeed. There are no cushions in the intermediate class, and the population are either intermediate, which is Eurasian, or native, which for a long night journey is nasty, or loafer, which is amusing though intoxicated. Intermediates do not patronize refreshment rooms. They carry their food in bundles and pots, and buy sweets from the native sweet-meat sellers, and drink the roadside water. That is why in the hot weather intermediates are taken out of the carriages dead, and in all weathers are most properly looked down upon.

My particular intermediate happened to be empty till I reached Nasirabad, when a huge gentleman in shirt sleeves entered, and, following the custom of intermediates, passed the time of day. He was a wanderer and a vagabond like myself, but with an educated taste for whiskey. He told tales of things he had seen and done, of out-of-the-way corners of the empire into which he had penetrated, and of adventures in which he risked his life for a few days' food. "If India was filled with men like you and me, not knowing more than the crows where they'd get their next day's rations, it isn't seventy millions of revenue the land would be paying—it's seven hundred millions," said he; and as I looked at his mouth and chin I was disposed to agree with him. We talked politics—the politics of loaferdom that sees things from the underside where the lath and plaster is not smoothed off—and we talked postal arrangements because my friend wanted to send a telegram back from the next station to Ajmir, which is the turning-off place from the Bombay to the Mhow line as you travel westward. My friend had no money beyond eight annas which he wanted for dinner, and I had no money at all, owing to the hitch in the budget before mentioned. Further, I was going into a wilderness where, though I should resume touch with the treasury, there were no telegraph offices, I was, therefore, unable to help him in any way.

"We might threaten a stationmaster, and make him send a wire on tick," said my friend, "but that'd mean inquiries for you and for me, and I've got my hands full these days. Did you say you are traveling back along this line within any days?"

"Within ten," I said.

"Can't you make it eight?" said he. "Mine is rather urgent business."

"I can send your telegram within ten days if that will serve you," I said.

"I couldn't trust the wire to fetch him now I think of it. It's this way. He leaves Delhi on the 23rd for Bombay. That means he'll be running through Ajmir about the night of the 23rd."

"But I am going into the Indian Desert," I explained.

"Well and good," said he. "You'll be changing at Marwar Junction to get into Jodhpore territory—you must do that—and he'll be coming through Marwar Junction in the early morning of the 24th by the Bombay Mail. Can you be at Marwar Junction on that time? 'Twon't be inconveniencing you because I know that there's precious few pickings to be got out of these Central India States—even though you pretend to be correspondent of the *Backwoodsman*."

"Have you ever tried that trick?" I asked.

"Again and again, but the residents find you out, and then you get escorted to the border before you've time to get your knife into them. But about my friend here. I *must* give him a word o' mouth to tell him what's come to me or else he won't know where to go. I would take it more than kind of you if you was to come out of Central India in time to catch him at Marwar Junction, and say to him: 'He has gone south for the week.' He'll know what that means. He's a big man with a red beard, and a great swell he is. You'll find him sleeping like a gentleman with all his luggage round him in a second-class compartment. But don't you be afraid. Slip down the window, and say: 'He has gone south for the week,' and he'll tumble. It's only cutting your time of stay in those parts by two days. I ask you as a stranger—going to the West," he said, with emphasis.

"Where have *you* come from?" said I.

"From the East," said he, "and I am hoping that you will give him the message on the square —for the sake of my mother as well as your own."

Englishmen are not usually softened by appeals to the memory of their mothers, but for certain reasons, which will be fully apparent, I saw fit to agree.

"It's more than a little matter," said he, "and that's why I ask you to do it—and now I know that I can depend on you doing it. A second-class carriage at Marwar Junction, and a red-haired man asleep in it. You'll be sure to remember. I get out at the next station, and I must hold on there till he comes or sends me what I want."

"I'll give the message if I catch him," I said,

4

"and for the sake of your mother as well as mine I'll give you a word of advice. Don't try to run the Central India States just now as the correspondent of the *Backwoodsman*. There's a real one knocking about here, and it might lead to trouble."

"Thank you," said he, simply, "and when will the swine be gone? I can't starve because he's running my work. I wanted to get hold of the Degumber Rajah down here about his father's widow, and give him a jump."

"What did he do to his father's widow, then?"

"Filled her up with red pepper and slippered her to death as she hung from a beam. I found that out myself and I'm the only man that would dare going into the State to get hush money for it. They'll try to poison me, same as they did in Chortumna when I went on the loot there. But you'll give the man at Marwar Junction my message?"

He got out at a little roadside station, and I reflected. I had heard, more than once, of men personating correspondents of newspapers and bleeding small Native States with threats of exposure, but I had never met any of the caste before. They lead a hard life, and generally die with great suddenness. The Native States have a wholesome horror of English newspapers, which may throw light on their peculiar methods of government, and do their best to choke correspondents with champagne, or drive them out of their mind with four-in-hand barouches. They do not understand that nobody cares a straw for the internal administration of Native States so long as

5

oppression and crime are kept within decent limits, and the ruler is not drugged, drunk, or diseased from one end of the year to the other. Native States were created by Providence in order to supply picturesque scenery, tigers, and tall writing. They are the dark places of the earth, full of unimaginable cruelty, touching the railway and the telegraph on one side, and, on the other, the days of Harun-al-Raschid. When I left the train I did business with divers kings, and in eight days passed through many changes of life. Sometimes I wore dress clothes and consorted with princes and politicals, drinking from crystal and eating from silver. Sometimes I lay out upon the ground and devoured what I could get, from a plate made of a flapjack, and drank the running water, and slept under the same rug as my servant. It was all in the day's work.

Then I headed for the Great Indian Desert upon the proper date, as I had promised, and the Night Mail set me down at Marwar Junction, where a funny little, happy-go-lucky, native-managed railway runs to Jodhpore. The Bombay Mail from Delhi makes a short halt at Marwar. She arrived as I got in, and I had just time to hurry to her platform and go down the carriages. There was only one second class on the train. I slipped the window and looked down upon a flaming red beard, half covered by a railway rug. That was my man, fast asleep, and I dug him gently in the ribs. He woke with a grunt and I saw his face in the light of the lamps. It was a great and shining face.

"Tickets again?" said he.

"No," said I. "I am to tell you that he is gone south for the week. He is gone south for the week!"

The train had begun to move out. The red man rubbed his eyes. "He has gone south for the week," he repeated. "Now that's just like his impudence. Did he say that I was to give you anything?—'Cause I won't."

"He didn't," I said, and dropped away, and watched the red lights die out in the dark. It was horribly cold because the wind was blowing off the sands. I climbed into my own train—not an intermediate carriage this time—and went to sleep.

If the man with the beard had given me a rupee I should have kept it as a memento of a rather curious affair. But the consciousness of having done my duty was my only reward.

Later on I reflected that two gentlemen like my friends could not do any good if they foregathered and personated correspondents of newspapers, and might, if they "stuck up" one of the little rat-trap states of Central India or Southern Rajputana, get themselves into serious difficulties. I therefore took some trouble to describe them as accurately as I could remember to people who would be interested in deporting them: and succeeded, so I was later informed, in having them headed back from the Degumber border.

Then I became respectable, and returned to an office where there were no kings and no incidents except the daily manufacture of a newspaper. A newspaper office seems to attract every conceivable sort of person, to the prejudice of discipline.

Zenana-mission ladies arrive, and beg that the editor will instantly abandon all his duties to describe a Christian prize-giving in a back slum of a perfectly inaccessible village; colonels who have been over-passed for commands sit down and sketch the outline of a series of ten, twelve, or twenty-four leading articles on seniority *versus* selection; missionaries wish to know why they have not been permitted to escape from their regular vehicles of abuse and swear at a brother-missionary under special patronage of the editorial We; stranded theatrical companies troop up to explain that they cannot pay for their advertisements, but on their return from New Zealand or Tahiti will do so with interest; inventors of patent punkah-pulling machines, carriage couplings and unbreakable swords and axle trees call with specifications in their pockets and hours at their disposal; tea companies enter and elaborate their prospectuses with the office pens; secretaries of ball committees clamor to have the glories of their last dance more fully expounded; strange ladies rustle in and say: "I want a hundred lady's cards printed *at once*, please," which is manifestly part of an editor's duty; and every dissolute ruffian that ever tramped the Grand Trunk Road makes it his business to ask for employment as a proofreader. And, all the time, the telephone bell is ringing madly, and kings are being killed on the continent, and empires are saying—"You're another," and Mister Gladstone is calling down brimstone upon the British dominions, and the little black copy boys are whining, *"kaa-pi chay-ha-yeh"* (copy wanted) like tired bees, and most of the paper is as blank as Modred's shield.

But that is the amusing part of the year. There are other six months wherein none ever come to call, and the thermometer walks inch by inch up to the top of the glass, and the office is darkened to just above reading light, and the press machines are red-hot of touch, and nobody writes anything but accounts of amusements in the hill stations or obituary notices. Then the telephone becomes a tinkling terror, because it tells you of the sudden deaths of men and women that you knew intimately, and the prickly heat covers you as with a garment, and you sit down and write: "A slight increase of sickness is reported from the Khuda Janta Khan district. The outbreak is purely sporadic in its nature, and, thanks to the energetic efforts of the district authorities, is now almost at an end. It is, however, with deep regret we record the death, etc."

Then the sickness really breaks out, and the less recording and reporting the better for the peace of the subscribers. But the empires and the kings continue to divert themselves as selfishly as before, and the foreman thinks that a daily paper really ought to come out once in twenty-four hours, and all the people at the hill stations in the middle of their amusements say: "Good gracious! Why can't the paper be sparkling? I'm sure there's plenty going on up here."

That is the dark half of the moon, and, as the advertisements say, "must be experienced to be appreciated."

It was in that season, and a remarkably evil

season, that the paper began running the last issue of the week on Saturday night, which is to say Sunday morning, after the custom of a London paper. This was a great convenience, for immediately after the paper was put to bed, the dawn would lower the thermometer from 96° to almost 84° for half an hour, and in that chill—you have no idea how cold is 84° on the grass until you begin to pray for it—a very tired man could set off to sleep ere the heat roused him.

One Saturday night it was my pleasant duty to put the paper to bed alone. A king or courtier or a courtesan or a community was going to die or get a new constitution, or do something that was important on the other side of the world, and the paper was to be held open till the latest possible minute in order to catch the telegram. It was a pitchy black night, as stifling as a June night can be, and the *loo*, the red-hot wind from the westward, was booming among the tinder-dry trees and pretending that the rain was on its heels. Now and again a spot of almost boiling water would fall on the dust with the flop of a frog, but all our weary world knew that was only pretense. It was a shade cooler in the press room than the office, so I sat there, while the type ticked and clicked, and the nightjars hooted at the windows, and the all but naked compositors wiped the sweat from their foreheads and called for water. The thing that was keeping us back, whatever it was, would not come off, though the *loo* dropped and the last type was set, and the whole round earth stood still in the choking heat, with its finger on its lip, to wait the event. I drowsed, and wondered whether the telegraph was a blessing, and whether this dying man, or struggling people, was aware of the inconvenience the delay was causing. There was no special reason beyond the heat and worry to make tension, but, as the clock hands crept up to three o'clock and the machines spun their flywheels two and three times to see that all was in order, before I said the word that would set them off, I could have shrieked aloud.

Then the roar and rattle of the wheels shivered the quiet into little bits. I rose to go away, but two men in white clothes stood in front of me. The first one said: "It's him!" The second said: "So it is!" And they both laughed almost as loudly as the machinery roared, and mopped their foreheads. "We see there was a light burning across the road and we were sleeping in that ditch there for coolness, and I said to my friend here, "The office is open. Let's come along and speak to him as turned us back from the Degumber State," said the smaller of the two. He was the man I had met in the Mhow train, and his fellow was the red-bearded man of Marwar Junction. There was no mistaking the eyebrows of the one or the beard of the other.

I was not pleased, because I wished to go to sleep, not to squabble with loafers. "What do you want?" I asked.

"Half an hour's talk with you cool and comfortable, in the office," said the red-bearded man. "We'd *like* some drink—the contrack doesn't begin yet, Peachey, so you needn't look—but what we really want is advice. We don't want money. We ask you as a favor, because you did us a bad turn about Degumber."

I led from the press room to the stifling office with the maps on the walls, and the red-haired man rubbed his hands. "That's something like," said he. "This was the proper shop to come to. Now, sir, let me introduce to you Brother Peachey Carnehan, that's him, and Brother Daniel Dravot, that is *me,* and the less said about our professions the better, for we have been most things in our time. Soldier, sailor, compositor, photographer, proofreader, street-preacher, and correspondents of the *Backwoodsman* when we thought the paper wanted one. Carnehan is sober, and so am I. Look at us first and see that's sure. It will save you cutting into my talk. We'll take one of your cigars apiece, and you shall see us light."

I watched the test. The men were absolutely sober, so I gave them each a tepid peg.

"Well *and* good," said Carnehan of the eyebrows, wiping the froth from his mustache. "Let me talk now, Dan. We have been all over India, mostly on foot. We have been boiler-fitters, engine-drivers, petty contractors, and all that, and we have decided that India isn't big enough for such as us."

They certainly were too big for the office. Dravot's beard seemed to fill half the room and Carnehan's shoulders the other half, as they sat on the big table. Carnehan continued: "The country isn't half worked out because they that governs it won't let you touch it. They spend all their blessed time in governing it, and you can't lift a spade, nor chip a rock, nor look for oil, nor anything like that without all the government saying—'Leave it alone and let us govern.' Therefore, such as it is, we will let it alone, and go away to some other place where a man isn't crowded and can come to his own. We are not little men, and there is nothing that we are afraid of except drink, and we have signed a contrack on that. *Therefore*, we are going away to be kings."

"Kings in our own right," muttered Dravot.

"Yes, of course," I said. "You've been tramping in the sun, and it's a very warm night, and hadn't you better sleep over the notion? Come tomorrow."

"Neither drunk nor sunstruck," said Dravot. "We have slept over the notion half a year, and require to see books and atlases, and we have decided that there is only one place now in the world that two strong men can Sar-a-*whack*. They call it Kafiristan. By my reckoning it's the top right-hand corner of Afghanistan, not more than three hundred miles from Peshawur. They have two and thirty heathen idols there, and we'll be the thirty-third. It's a mountainous country, and the women of those parts are very beautiful."

"But that is provided against in the contrack," said Carnehan. "Neither women nor liquor, Daniel."

"And that's all we know, except that no one has gone there, and they fight, and in any place where they fight a man who knows how to drill men can always be a king. We shall go to those parts and say to any king we find—'D' you want to vanquish your foes?' and we will show him how to drill men; for that we know better than anything else. Then we will subvert that king and seize his throne and establish a dynasty."

"You'll be cut to pieces before you're fifty miles across the border," I said. "You have to travel through Afghanistan to get to that country. It's one mass of mountains and peaks and glaciers, and no Englishman has been through it. The people are utter brutes, and even if you reached them you couldn't do anything."

"That's more like," said Carnehan. "If you could think us a little more mad we would be more pleased. We have come to you to know about this country, to read a book about it, and to be shown maps. We want you to tell us that we are fools and to show us your books." He turned to the bookcases.

"Are you at all in earnest?" I said.

"A little," said Dravot, sweetly. "As big a map as you have got, even if it's all blank where Kafiristan is, and any books you've got. We can read, though we aren't very educated."

I uncased the big thirty-two-miles-to-the-inch map of India, and two smaller frontier maps, hauled down volume INFKAN of the *Encyclopedia Britannica,* and the men consulted them.

"See here!" said Dravot, his thumb on the map. "Up to Jagdallak, Peachey and me know the road. We was there with Robert's Army. We'll have to turn off to the right at Jagdallak through Laghmann territory. Then we get among the hills—fourteen thousand feet— fifteen thousand—it will be cold work there, but it don't look very far on the map."

I handed him Wood on the *Sources of the Oxus.* Carnehan was deep in the *Encyclopedia.*

"They're a mixed lot," said Dravot, reflectively; "and it won't help us to know the names of their tribes. The more tribes the more they'll fight, and the better for us. From Jagdallak to Ashang. H'mm!"

"But all the information about the country is as sketchy and inaccurate as can be," I protested. "No one knows anything about it really. Here's the file of the *United Services' Institute*. Read what Bellew says."

"Blow Bellew!" said Carnehan. "Dan, they're an all-fired lot of heathens, but this book here says they think they're related to us English."

I smoked while the men pored over *Raverty*, *Wood*, the maps, and the *Encyclopedia*.

"There is no use your waiting," said Dravot, politely. "It's about four o'clock now. We'll go before six o'clock if you want to sleep, and we won't steal any of the papers. Don't you sit up. We're two harmless lunatics, and if you come, tomorrow evening, down to the Serai we'll say goodbye to you."

"You *are* two fools," I answered. "You'll be turned back at the frontier or cut up the minute you set foot in Afghanistan. Do you want any money or a recommendation down-country? I can help you to the chance of work next week."

"Next week we shall be hard at work ourselves, thank you," said Dravot. "It isn't so easy being a king as it looks. When we've got our kingdom in going order we'll let you know, and you can come up and help us to govern it."

"Would two lunatics make a contrack like that?" said Carnehan, with subdued pride, showing me a greasy half-sheet of note paper on which was written the following. I copied it, then and there, as a curiosity:

This contrack between me and you persuing witnesseth in the name of God—Amen and so forth.
- *(One)   That me and you will settle this matter together: i.e., to be kings of Kafiristan.*
- *(Two)   That you and me will not, while this matter is being settled, look at any liquor, nor any woman, black, white or brown, so as to get mixed up with one or the other harmful.*
- *(Three)   That we conduct ourselves with dignity and discretion, and if one of us gets into trouble the other will stay by him.*

Signed by you and me this day.
    Peachey Taliaferro Carnehan.
    Daniel Dravot.
    Both Gentlemen at Large.

"There was no need for the last article," said Carnehan, blushing modestly; "But it looks regular. Now you know the sort of men that loafers are—we *are* loafers, Dan, until we get out of India—and *do* you think that we would sign a contrack like that unless we was in earnest? We have kept away from the two things that make life worth having."

"You won't enjoy your lives much longer if you are going to try this idiotic adventure. Don't set the office on fire," I said, "and go away before nine o'clock."

I left them still poring over the maps and

making notes on the back of the "Contrack." "Be sure to come down to the Serai tomorrow," were their parting words.

The Kumharsen Serai is the great four-square sink of humanity where the strings of camels and horses from the North load and unload. All the nationalities of Central Asia may be found there, and most of the folk of India proper. Balkh and Bokhara there meet Bengal and Bombay, and try to draw eyeteeth. You can buy ponies, turquoises, Persian pussycats, saddlebags, fat-tailed sheep and musk in the Kumharsen Serai, and get many strange things for nothing. In the afternoon I went down there to see whether my friends intended to keep their word or were lying about drunk.

A priest attired in fragments of ribbons and rags stalked up to me, gravely twisting a child's paper whirligig. Behind him was his servant bending under the load of a crate of mud toys. The two were loading up two camels, and the inhabitants of the Serai watched them with shrieks of laughter.

"The priest is mad," said a horse dealer to me. "He is going up to Kabul to sell toys to the Amir. He will either be raised to honor or have his head cut off. He came in here this morning and has been behaving madly ever since."

"The witless are under the protection of God," stammered a flat-cheeked Usbeg in broken Hindi. "They foretell future events."

"Would they could have foretold that my caravan would have been cut up by the Shinwaris almost within shadow of the Pass!" grunted the Eusufzai agent of a Rajputana trading house whose goods had been feloniously diverted into the hands of other robbers just across the Border, and whose misfortunes were the laughingstock of the bazaar. "Ohé, priest, whence come you and whither do you go?"

"From Roum have I come," shouted the priest, waving his whirligig; "from Roum, blown by the breath of a hundred devils across the sea! O thieves, robbers, liars, the blessing of Pir Khan on pigs, dogs, and perjurers! Who will take the Protected of God to the North to sell charms that are never still to the Amir? The camels shall not gall, the sons shall not fall sick, and the wives shall remain faithful while they are away, of the men who give me place in their caravan. Who will assist me to slipper the King of the Roos with a golden slipper with a silver heel? The protection of Pir Khan be upon his labors!" He spread out the skirts of his gabardine and pirouetted between the lines of tethered horses.

"There starts a caravan from Peshawur to Kabul in twenty days, *Huzrut,*" said the Eusufzai trader. "My camels go therewith. Do thou also go and bring us good luck."

"I will go even now!" shouted the priest. "I will depart upon my winged camels, and be at Peshawur in a day! Ho! Hazar Mir Khan," he yelled to his servant, "drive out the camels, but let me first mount my own."

He leaped on the back of his beast as it knelt, and, turning round to me, cried: "Come thou also, Sahib, a little along the road and I will sell thee a charm—an amulet that shall make thee king of Kafiristan."

Then the light broke upon me and I followed the

two camels out of the Serai till we reached open road and the priest halted.

"What d' you think o' that?" said he in English. "Carnehan can't talk their patter, so I've made him my servant. He makes a handsome servant. 'Tisn't for nothing that I've been knocking about the country for fourteen years. Didn't I do that talk neat? We'll hitch on to a caravan at Peshawur till we get to Jagdallak, and then we'll see if we can get donkeys for our camels, and strike into Kafiristan. Whirligigs for the Amir, O Lor! Put your hand under the camel bags and tell me what you feel."

I felt the butt of a Martini, and another and another.

"Twenty of 'em," said Dravot, placidly. "Twenty of 'em, and ammunition to correspond, under the whirligigs and the mud dolls."

"Heaven help you if you are caught with those things!" I said. "A Martini is worth her weight in silver among the Pathans."

"Fifteen hundred rupees of capital—every rupee we could beg, borrow, or steal—are invested on these two camels," said Dravot. "We won't get caught. We're going through the Khyber with a regular caravan. Who'd touch a poor mad priest?"

"Have you got everything you want?" I asked, overcome with astonishment.

"Not yet, but we shall soon. Give us a memento of your kindness, brother. You did me a service yesterday, and that time in Marwar. Half my kingdom shall you have, as the saying is." I slipped a small charm compass from my watch chain and handed it up to the priest.

"Goodbye," said Dravot, giving me a hand cautiously. "It's the last time we'll shake hands with an Englishman these many days. Shake hands with him, Carnehan," he cried, as the second camel passed me.

Carnehan leaned down and shook hands. Then the camels passed away along the dusty road, and I was left alone to wonder. My eye could detect no failure in the disguises. The scene in Serai attested that they were complete to the native mind. There was just the chance, therefore, that Carnehan and Dravot would be able to wander through Afghanistan without detection. But, beyond, they would find death, certain and awful death.

Ten days later a native friend of mine, giving me the news of the day from Peshawur, wound up his letter with: "There has been much laughter here on account of a certain mad priest who is going to his estimation to sell petty gauds and insignificant trinkets which he ascribes as great charms to H.H. the Amir of Bokhara. He passed through Peshawur and associated himself to the Second Summer caravan that goes to Kabul. The merchants are pleased because through superstition they imagine that such mad fellows bring good fortune."

The two, then, were beyond the border. I would have prayed for them, but, that night, a real king died in Europe and demanded an obituary notice.

The wheel of the world swings through the same phases again and again. Summer passed and winter thereafter, and came and passed again. The daily paper continued and I with it, and upon the third summer there fell a hot night, a night issue, and a strained waiting for something to be telegraphed from the other side of the world, exactly as had happened before. A few great men had died in the past two years, the machines worked with more clatter, and some of the trees in the office garden were a few feet taller. But that was all the difference.

I passed over to the press room, and went through just such a scene as I have already described. The nervous tension was stronger than it had been two years before, and I felt the heat more acutely. At three o'clock I cried, "Print off," and turned to go, when there crept to my chair what was left of a man. He was bent into a circle, his head was sunk between his shoulders, and he moved his feet one over the other like a bear. I could hardly see whether he walked or crawled—this rag-wrapped, whining cripple who addressed me by name, crying that he was come back, "Can you give me a drink?" he whimpered. "For the Lord's sake, give me a drink!"

I went back to the office, the man following with groans of pain, and I turned up the lamp.

"Don't you know me?" he gasped, dropping into a chair, and he turned his drawn face, surmounted by a shock of gray hair, to the light.

I looked at him intently. Once before had I seen eyebrows that met over the nose in an inch-broad black band, but for the life of me I could not tell where.

"I don't know you," I said, handing him the whiskey. "What can I do for you?"

He took a gulp of the spirit raw, and shivered in spite of the suffocating heat.

"I've come back," he repeated; "and I was the King of Kafiristan—me and Dravot—crowned kings we was! In this office we settled it—you setting there and giving us the books. I am Peachey—Peachey Taliaferro Carnehan, and you've been setting here ever since—O Lord!"

I was more than a little astonished, and expressed my feelings accordingly.

"It's true," said Carnehan, with a dry cackle, nursing his feet, which were wrapped in rags. "True as gospel. Kings we were, with crowns upon our heads—me and Dravot—poor Dan—oh, poor, poor Dan, that would never take advice, not though I begged of him!"

"Take the whiskey," I said, "and take your own time. Tell me all you can recollect of everything from beginning to end. You got across the border on your camels, Dravot dressed as a mad priest and you his servant. Do you remember that?"

"I ain't mad—yet, but I shall be that way soon. Of course I remember. Keep looking at me, or maybe my words will go all to pieces. Keep looking at me in my eyes and don't say anything."

I leaned forward and looked into his face as steadily as I could. He dropped one hand upon the table and I grasped it by the wrist. It was twisted like a bird's claw, and upon the back was a ragged, red, diamond-shaped scar.

"No, don't look there. Look at *me*," said Carnehan.

"That comes afterward, but for the Lord's sake don't distrack me. We left with that caravan, me and Dravot playing all sorts of antics to amuse the people we were with. Dravot used to make us laugh in the evenings when all the people were cooking their dinners—cooking their dinners, and...what did they do then? They lit little fires with sparks that went into Dravot's beard, and we all laughed—fit to die. Little red fires they was, going into Dravot's big red beard—so funny." His eyes left mine and he smiled foolishly.

"You went as far as Jagdallak with that caravan," I said, at a venture, "after you had lit those fires. To Jagdallak, where you turned off to try to get into Kafiristan."

"No, we didn't neither. What are you talking about? We turned off before Jagdallak, because we heard the roads was good. But they wasn't good enough for our two camels—mine and Dravot's. When we left the caravan, Dravot took off all his clothes and mine too, and said we would be heathen, because the Kafirs didn't allow Mohammedans to talk to them. So we dressed betwixt and between, and such a sight as Daniel Dravot I never saw yet now expect to see again. He burned half his beard, and slung a sheepskin over his shoulder, and shaved his head into patterns. He shaved mine, too, and made me wear outrageous things to look like a heathen. That was in a most mountainous country and our camels couldn't go along anymore because of the mountains. They were tall and black, and coming home I saw them fight like wild goats—there are lots of goats in Kafiristan. And these mountains, they never keep still, no more than the goats. Always fighting they are, and don't let you sleep at night."

"Take some more whiskey," I said, very slowly. "What did you and Daniel Dravot do when the camels could go no further because of the rough roads that led into Kafiristan?''

"What did which do? There was a party called Peachey Taliaferro Carnehan that was with Dravot. Shall I tell you about him? He died out there in the cold. Slap from the bridge fell old Peachey, turning and twisting in the air like a penny whirligig that you can sell to the Amir.— No; they was two for three ha'pence, those whirligigs, or I am much mistaken and woeful sore. And then these camels were no use, and Peachey said to Dravot—'For the Lord's sake, let's get out of this before our heads are chopped off,' and with that they killed the camels all among the mountains, not having anything in particular to eat, but first they took off the boxes with the guns and the ammunition, till two men came along driving four mules. Dravot up and dances in front of them, singing, 'Sell me four mules.' Says the first man, 'If you are rich enough to buy, you are rich enough to rob'; but before ever he could put his hand to his knife, Dravot breaks his neck over his knee, and the other party runs away. So Carnehan loaded the mules with the rifles that was taken off the camels, and together we starts forward into those bitter cold mountainous parts, and never a road broader than the back of your hand.''

He paused for a moment, while I asked him if he could remember the nature of the country through which he had journeyed.

"I am telling you as straight as I can, but my head isn't as good as it might be. They drove nails through it to make me hear better how Dravot died. The country was mountainous and the mules were most contrary, and the inhabitants was dispersed and solitary. They went up and up, and down and down, and that other party, Carnehan, was imploring of Dravot not to sing and whistle so loud, for fear of bringing down the tremenjus avalanches. But Dravot says that if a king couldn't sing it wasn't worth being king, and whacked the mules over the rump, and never took no heed for ten cold days. We came to a big level valley all among the mountains, and the mules were near dead, so we killed them, not having anything in special for them or us to eat. We sat upon the boxes, and played odds and even with the cartridges that was jolted out.

"Then ten men with bows and arrows ran down that valley, chasing twenty men with bows and arrows, and the row was tremenjus. They were fair men—fairer than you or me—with yellow hair and remarkable well built. Says Dravot, unpacking the guns—"This is the beginning of the business. We'll fight for the ten men," and with that he fires two rifles at the twenty men, and drops one of them at two hundred yards from the rock where we was sitting. The other men began to run but Carnehan and Dravot sits on the boxes picking them off at all ranges, up and down the valley. Then we goes up to the ten men that had run across the snow too, and they fires a footy little arrow at us. Dravot he shoots above their heads and they all falls down flat. Then he walks over them and kicks them, and then he lifts them up and shakes hands all round to make them friendly like. He calls them and gives them the boxes to carry, and waves his hand for all the world as though he was king already. They takes the boxes and him across the valley and up the hill into a pine wood on the top, where there was half a dozen big stone idols. Dravot he goes to the biggest—a fellow they call Imbra—and lays a rifle and cartridge at his feet, rubbing his nose respectful with his own nose, patting him on the head, and saluting in front of it. He turns round to the men and nods his head, and says, 'That's all right. I'm in the know too, and all these old jim-jams are my friends.' Then he opens his mouth and points down it, and when the first man brings him food, he says—'No'; and when the second man brings him food, he says 'No'; but when one of the old priests and the boss of the village brings him food, he says—'Yes'; very haughty, and eats it slow. That was how we came to our first village, without any trouble, just as though we had tumbled from the skies. But we tumbled from one of those damned rope-bridges, you see, and you couldn't expect a man to laugh much after that.''

''Take some more whiskey and go on,'' I said. ''That was the first village you came into. How did you get to be king?''

''I wasn't king,'' said Carnehan. ''Dravot he was the king, and a handsome man he looked with the gold crown on his head and all. Him and the other party stayed in that village, and every morning Dravot sat by the side of old Imbra, and the people came and worshiped. That was Dravot's order. Then a lot of men came into the valley, and Carnehan and Dravot picks them off with the rifles before they knew where they was, and runs down into the valley and up again the other side, and finds another village, same as the first one, and the people all falls down flat on their faces, and Dravot says, 'Now what is the trouble between you two villages?' and the people points to a woman, as fair as you or me, that was carried off, and Dravot takes her back to the first village and counts up the dead—eight there was. For each dead man Dravot pours a little milk on the ground and waves his arms like a whirligig and 'That's all right,' says he. Then he and Carnehan takes the big boss of each village by the arm and walks them down into the valley, and shows them how to scratch a line with a spear right down the valley, and gives each a sod of turf from both sides o' the line. Then all the people comes down and shouts like the devil and all, and Dravot says, 'Go and dig the land, and be fruitful and multiply,' which they did, though they didn't understand. Then we asks the names of things in their lingo—bread and water and fire and idols and such, and Dravot leads the priest of each village up to the idol, and says he must sit there and judge the people, and if anything goes wrong he is to be shot.

"Next week they was all turning up the land in the valley as quiet as bees and much prettier, and the priests heard all the complaints and told Dravot in dumb show what it was about. 'That's just the beginning,' said Dravot. 'They think we're gods.' He and Carnehan picks out twenty good men and shows them how to click off a rifle, and form fours, and advance in line, and they was very pleased to do so, and clever to see the hang of it. Then he takes out his pipe and his baccy pouch and leaves one at one village and one at the other, and off we two goes to see what was to be done in the next valley. That was all rock, and there was a little village there, and

Carnehan says, 'Send 'em to the old valley to plant,' and takes 'em there and gives 'em some land that wasn't took before. They were a poor lot, and we blooded 'em with a kid before letting 'em into the new kingdom. That was to impress the people, and then they settled down quiet and, Carnehan went back to Dravot who had got into another valley, all snow and ice and most mountainous. There was no people there and the army got afraid, so Dravot shoots one of them, and goes on till he finds some people in a village, and the army explains that unless the people wants to be killed they had better not shoot their little match-locks; for they had matchlocks. We make friends with the priest and I stays there alone with two of the army, teaching the men how to drill, and a thundering big chief comes across the snow with kettledrums and horns twanging, because he heard there was a new god kicking about. Carnehan sights for the brown of the men half a mile across the snow and wings one of them. Then he sends a message to the chief that, unless he wished to be killed, he must come and shake hands with me and leave his arms behind. The chief comes alone first, and Carnehan shakes hands with him and whirls his arms about, same as Dravot used, and very much surprised that chief was, and strokes my eyebrows. Then Carnehan goes alone to the chief, and asks him in dumb show if he had an enemy he hated. 'I have,' says the chief. So Carnehan weeds out the pick of his men, and sets the two of the army to show them drill and at the end of two weeks the men can maneuver about as well as volunteers. So he marches with the chief to a great big plain on the top of a mountain, and the chief's men rushes into a village and takes it; we three Martinis firing into the brown of the enemy. So we took that village too, and I gives the chief a rag from my coat and says, 'Occupy till I come': which was scriptural. By way of a reminder, when me and the army was eighteen hundred yards away, I drops a bullet near him standing on the snow, and all the people falls flat on their faces. Then I sends a letter to Dravot, wherever he be by land or by sea.''

At the risk of throwing the creature out of train I interrupted, "How could you write a letter up yonder?"

"The letter? Oh! The letter! Keep looking at me between the eyes, please. It was a string-talk letter, that we'd learned the way of it from a blind beggar in the Punjab."

I remember that there had once come to the office a blind man with a knotted twig and a piece of string which he wound round the twig according to some cipher of his own. He could, after the lapse of days or hours, repeat the sentence which he had reeled up. He had reduced the alphabet to eleven primitive sounds; and tried to teach me his method, but failed.

"I sent that letter to Dravot," said Carnehan; "and told him to come back because this kingdom was growing too big for me to handle, and then I struck for the first valley, to see how the priests were working. They called the village we took along with the chief, Bashkai, and the first village we took, Er-Heb. The priests at Er-Heb were doing all right, but they had a lot of pending cases about land to show me, and some men from another village had been firing arrows at night. I went out and looked for that village and fired four rounds at it from a thousand yards. That used all the cartridges I cared to spend, and I waited for Dravot, who had been away two or three months, and I kept my people quiet.

"One morning I heard the devil's own noise of drums and horns, and Dan Dravot marches down the hill with his army and a tail of hundreds of men, and, which was the most amazing—a great gold crown on his head. 'My Gord, Carnehan,' says Daniel, 'this is a tremendjus business, and we've got the whole country as far as it's worth having. I am the son of Alexander by Queen Semiramis, and you're my younger brother and a god, too! It's the biggest thing we've ever seen. I've been marching and fighting for six weeks with the army, and every footy little village for fifty miles has come in rejoiceful; and more than that, I've got the key of the whole show, as you'll see, and I've got a crown for you! I told 'em to make two of 'em at a place called Shu, where the gold lies in the rock like suet in mutton. Gold I've seen, and turquoise I've kicked out of the cliffs, and there's garnets in the sands of the river, and here's a chunk of amber that a man brought me. Call up all the priests and, here, take your crown.'

"One of the men opens a black hair bag and I slips the crown on. It was too small and too heavy, but I wore it for the glory. Hammered gold it was— five pound weight, like a hoop of a barrel.

"'Peachey,' says Dravot, 'we don't want to fight no more. The craft's the trick so help me!' and he brings forward the same chief that I left at

Bashkai—Billy Fish we called him afterward, because he was so like Billy Fish that drove the big tank-engine at Mach on the Bolan in the old days. 'Shake hands with him,' says Dravot, and I shook hands and nearly dropped, for Billy Fish gave me the grip. I said nothing, but tried him with the fellow craft grip. He answers, all right, and I tried the master's grip, but that was a slip. 'A fellow craft he is!' I says to Dan. 'Does he know the word?' 'He does,' says Dan, 'and all the priests know. It's a miracle! The chiefs and the priests can work a fellow craft lodge in a way that's very like ours, and they've cut the marks on the rocks, but they don't know the third degree, and they've come to find out. It's Gord's truth. I've known these long years that the Afghans knew up to the fellow craft degree, but this is a miracle. A god and a grand master of the craft am I, and a lodge in the third degree I will open, and we'll raise the head priests and the chiefs of the villages.'

" 'It's against all the law,' I says, 'holding a lodge without warrant from anyone; and we never held office in any lodge.'

" 'It's a masterstroke of policy,' says Dravot. 'It means running the country as easy as a four-wheeled bogie on a downgrade. We can't stop to inquire now, or they'll turn against us. I've forty chiefs at my heel, and passed and raised according to their merit they shall be. Billet these men on the villages and see that we run up a lodge of some kind. The temple of Imbra will do for the lodge room. The women must make aprons as you show them. I'll hold a levee of chiefs tonight and lodge tomorrow.'

"I was fair run off my legs, but I wasn't such a fool as not to see what a pull this craft business gave us. I showed the priests' families how to make aprons of the degrees, but for Dravot's apron the blue border and marks was made of turquoise lumps on white hide, not cloth. We took a great square stone in the temple for the master's chair, and little stones for the officers' chairs, and painted the black pavement with white squares, and did what we could to make things regular.

"At the levee which was held that night on the hillside with big bonfires, Dravot gives out that him and me were gods and sons of Alexander, and past grand masters in the craft, and was come to make Kafiristan a country where every man should eat in peace and drink in quiet, and specially obey us. Then the chiefs come round to shake hands, and they was so hairy and white and fair it was just shaking hands with old friends. We gave them names according as they was like men we had known in India—Billy Fish, Holly Dilworth, Pikky Kergan that was bazaar master when I was at Mhow, and so on and so on.

"The *most* amazing miracle was at lodge next night. One of the old priests was watching us continuous, and I felt uneasy, for I knew we'd have to fudge the ritual, and I didn't know what the men knew. The old priest was a stranger come in from beyond the village of Bashkai. The minute Dravot puts on the master's apron that the girls had made for him, the priest fetches a whoop and a howl, and tries to overturn the stone that Dravot was sitting on. 'It's all up now,' I says. 'That comes of meddling with the craft without warrant!' Dravot never winked an eye, not when ten priests took and tilted over the grand master's chair—which was to say the stone of Imbra. The priest begins rubbing the bottom end of it to clear away the black dirt, and presently he shows all the other priests the master's mark, same as was on Dravot's apron, cut into the stone. Not even the priests of the temple of Imbra knew it was there. The old chap falls flat on his face at Dravot's feet and kisses 'em. 'Luck again,' says Dravot, across the lodge to me, 'they say it's the missing mark that no one could understand the why of. We're more than safe now.' Then he bangs the butt of his gun for a gavel and says: 'By virtue of the authority vested in me by my own right hand and the help of Peachey, I declare myself grand master of all Freemasonry in Kafiristan in this the mother lodge o' the country, and the King of Kafiristan equally with Peachey!' At that he puts on his crown and I puts on mine—I was doing senior warden—and we opens the lodge in most ample form. It was an amazing miracle! The priests moved in lodge through the first two degrees almost without telling, as if the memory was coming back to them. After that, Peachey and Dravot raised such as was worthy—high priests and chiefs of far-off villages. Billy Fish was the first, and I can tell you we scared the soul out of him. It was not in any way according to ritual, but it served our turn. We didn't raise more than ten of the biggest men because we didn't want to make the degree common. And they was clamoring to be raised.

"'In another six months,' says Dravot, 'we'll hold another communication and see how you are working.' Then he asks them about their villages, and learns that they was fighting one against the other and were fair sick and tired of it. And when they wasn't doing that, they was fighting with the Mohammedans. 'You can fight those when they come into our country,' says Dravot. 'Tell off every tenth man of your tribes for a frontier guard, and send two hundred at a time to this valley to be drilled. Nobody is going to be shot or speared anymore so long as he does well, and I know that you won't cheat me because you're white people—sons of Alexander—and not like common, black Mohammedans. You are *my* people and by God,' says he, running off into English at the end—'I'll make a damned fine nation of you, or I'll die in the making!'

"I can't tell all we did for the next six months because Dravot did a lot I couldn't see the hang of, and he learned their lingo in a way I never could. My work was to help the people plough, and now and again go out with some of the army and see what the other villages were doing, and make 'em throw rope bridges across the ravines which cut up the country horrid. Dravot was very kind to me, but when he walked up and down in the pine wood pulling that bloody red beard of his with both fists I knew he was thinking plans I could not advise him about, and I just waited for orders.

"But Dravot never showed me disrespect before the people. They were afraid of me and the army, but they loved Dan. He was the best of friends with the priests and the chiefs; but anyone could come across the hills with a complaint and Dravot would hear him out fair, and call four priests together and say what was to be done. He used to call in Billy Fish from Bashkai, and Pikky Kergan from Shu, and an old chief we called Kafuzelum—it was like enough to his real name—and hold councils with 'em when there was any fighting to be done in small villages. That was his council of war, and the four priests of Bashkai, Shu, Khawak, and Madora was his privy council. Between the lot of 'em they send me, with forty men and twenty rifles, and sixty men carrying turquoises, into the Ghorband country to buy those handmade Martini rifles, that come out of the Amir's workshops at Kabul, from one of the Amir's Herati regiments that would have sold the very teeth out of their mouth for turquoises.

"I stayed in Ghorband a month, and gave the governor there the pick of my baskets for hush money, and bribed the colonel of the regiment some more, and, between the two and the tribespeople, we got more than a hundred handmade Martinis, a hundred good Kohat Jezails, that'll throw to six hundred yards, and forty man-loads of very bad ammunition for the rifles. I came back with what I had, and distributed 'em among the men that the chiefs sent to me to drill. Dravot was too busy to attend to those things, but the old army that we first made helped me, and we turned out five hundred men that could drill, and two hundred that knew how to hold arms pretty straight. Even those corkscrewed, handmade guns was a miracle to them. Dravot talked big about powder shops and factories, walking up and down in the pine wood when the winter was coming on.

"'I won't make a nation,' says he, 'I'll make an

empire! These men aren't Negroes; they're English! Look at their eyes—look at their mouths. Look at the way they stand up. They sit on chairs in their own houses. They're the Lost Tribes, or something like it, and they've grown to be English. I'll take a census in the spring if the priests don't get frightened. There must be a fair two million of 'em in these hills. The villages are full o' little children. Two million people—two hundred and fifty thousand fighting men—and all English! They only want the rifles and a little drilling. Two hundred and fifty thousand men, ready to cut in on Russia's right flank when she tries for India! Peachey, man,' he says, chewing his beard in great hunks, 'we shall be emperors—emperors of the Earth! Rajah Brooke will be a suckling to us. I'll treat with the viceroy on equal terms. I'll ask him to send me twelve picked English—twelve that I know of—to help us govern a bit. There's Mackray, sergeant-pensioner at Segowli—many's the good dinner he's given me, and his wife a pair of trousers. There's Donkin, the warder of Tounghoo Jail; there's hundreds that I could lay my hand on if I was in India. The viceroy shall do it for me. I'll send a man through in the spring for those men, and I'll write for a dispensation from the grand lodge for what I've done as grand master. That—and all the Sniders that'll be thrown out when the native troops in India take up the Martini. They'll be worn smooth, but they'll do for fighting in these hills. Twelve English, a hundred thousand sniders run through the Amir's country in driblets—I'd be content with twenty thousand in one year—and we'd be an empire. When everything was shipshape, I'd hand over the crown—this crown I'm wearing now—to Queen Victoria on my knees, and she'd say: "Rise up, Sir Daniel Dravot." Oh, it's big! It's big, I tell you! But there's so much to be done in every place—Bashkai, Khawak, Shu, and everywhere else.'

"'What is it?' I says. 'There are no more men coming in to be drilled this autumn. Look at those fat, black clouds. They're bringing the snow.'

"'It isn't that,'' says Daniel, putting his hand very hard on my shoulder; 'and I don't wish to say anything that's against you, for no other living man would have followed me and made me what I am as you have done. You're a first-class commander-in-chief, and the people know you; but—it's a big country, and somehow you can't help me, Peachey, in the way I want to be helped.'

"'Go to your blasted priests then!' I said, and I was sorry when I made that remark, but it did hurt me sore to find Daniel talking so superior when I'd drilled all the men, and done all he told me.

"'Don't let's quarrel, Peachey,' says Daniel, without cursing. 'You're a king too, and the half of this kingdom is yours; but can't you see, Peachey, we want cleverer men than us now—three or four of 'em, that we can scatter about for our deputies. It's a hugeous great state, and I can't always tell the right thing to do, and I haven't time for all I want to do, and here's the winter coming on and all.' He put half his beard into his mouth, and it was as red as the gold of his crown.

"'I'm sorry, Daniel,' says I. 'I've done all I could. I've drilled the men and shown the people how to stack their oats better; and I've brought in those tinware rifles from Ghorband—but I know what you're driving at. I take it kings always feel oppressed that way.'

" 'There's another thing too,' says Dravot, walking up and down. 'The winter's coming and these people won't be giving much trouble, and if they do we can't move about. I want a wife.'

" 'For God's sake leave the women alone!' I says. 'We've both got all the work we can, though I *am* a fool. Remember the contrack, and keep clear o' women.'

" 'The contrack only lasted till such time as we was kings; and kings we have been these months past,' says Dravot, weighing his crown in his hand. 'You go get a wife too, Peachey—a nice, strappin', plump girl that'll keep you warm in the winter. They're prettier than English girls, and we can take the pick of 'em. Boil 'em once or twice in hot water, and they'll come as fair as chicken and ham.'

" 'Don't tempt me!' I says. 'I will not have any dealings with a woman not till we are a dam' side more settled than we are now. I've been doing the work o' two men, and you've been doing the work o' three. Let's lie off a bit, and see if we can get some better tobacco from Afghan country and run in some good liquor; but no women.'

" 'Who' talking o' *women?*' says Dravot. 'I said *wife*—a queen to breed a king's son for the king. A queen out of the strongest tribe, that'll make them your blood brothers, and that'll lie by your side and tell you all the people thinks about you and their own affairs. That's what I want.'

" 'Do you remember that Bengali woman I kept at Mogul Serai when I was a plate-layer?' says I.

'A fat lot o' good she was to me. She taught me the lingo and one or two other things; but what happened? She ran away with the stationmaster's servant and half my month's pay. Then she turned up at Dadur Junction in tow of a half-caste, and had the impidence to say I was her husband—all among the drivers in the running shed!'

" 'We've done with that,' says Dravot. 'These women are whiter than you or me, and a queen I will have for the winter months.'

" 'For the last time o' asking, Dan, do *not*,' I says. 'It'll only bring us harm. The Bible says that kings ain't to waste their strength on women, 'specially when they've got a new raw kingdom to work over.'

" 'For the last time of answering I will,' said Dravot, and he went away through the pine trees looking like a big red devil. The low sun hit his crown and beard on one side and the two blazed like hot coals.

"But getting a wife was not as easy as Dan thought. He put it before the council, and there was no answer till Billy Fish said that he'd better ask the girls. Dravot damned them all round. 'What's wrong with me?' he shouts, standing by the idol Imbra. 'Am I a dog or am I not enough of a man for your wenches? Haven't I put the shadow of my hand over this country? Who stopped the last Afghan raid?' It was me really, but Dravot was too angry to remember. 'Who brought your guns? Who repaired the bridges? Who's the grand master of the sign cut in the stone?' and he thumped his hand on the block that he used to sit on in lodge, and at council, which opened like lodge always.

Billy Fish said nothing and no more did the others. 'Keep your hair on, Dan,' said I; 'and ask the girls. That's how it's done at home, and these people are quite English.'

" 'The marriage of the king is a matter of state,' says Dan, in a white-hot rage, for he could feel, I hope, that he was going against his better mind. He walked out of the council room, and the others sat still, looking at the ground.

" 'Billy Fish,' says I to the chief of Bashkai, 'what's the difficulty here? A straight answer to a true friend.' 'You know,' says Billy Fish. 'How should a man tell you who knows everything? How can daughters of men marry gods or devils? It's not proper.'

"I remember something like that in the Bible; but, if, after seeing us as long as they had they still believed we were gods, it wasn't for me to undeceive them.

" 'A god can do anything,' says I. 'If the king is fond of a girl he'll not let her die.' 'She'll have to,' said Billy Fish. 'There are all sorts of gods and devils in these mountains, and now and again a girl marries one of them and isn't seen anymore. Besides, you two know the mark cut in the stone. Only the gods know that. We thought you were men till you showed the sign of the master.'

"I wished then that we had explained about the loss of the genuine secrets of a master mason at the first go-off; but I said nothing. All that night there was a blowing of horns in a little dark temple half-way down the hill, and I heard a girl crying fit to die. One of the priests told us that she was being prepared to marry the king.

" 'I'll have no nonsense of that kind,' says Dan. 'I don't want to interfere with your customs, but I'll take my own wife.' 'The girl's a little bit afraid,' says the priest. 'She thinks she's going to die, and they are a-heartening of her up down in the temple.'

" 'Hearten her very tender, then,' says Dravot, 'or I'll hearten you with the butt of a gun so that you'll never want to be heartened again.' He licked his lips, did Dan, and stayed up walking about more than half the night, thinking of the wife that he was going to get in the morning. I wasn't any means comfortable, for I knew that dealings with a woman in foreign parts, though you was a crowned king twenty times over, could not but be risky. I got up very early in the morning while Dravot was asleep, and I saw the priests talking together in whispers, and the chiefs talking together too, and they looked at me out of the corners of their eyes.

" 'What is up, Fish?' I says to the Bashkai man, who was wrapped up in his furs and looking splendid to behold.

" 'I can't rightly say,' says he; 'but if you can induce the king to drop all this nonsense about marriage, you'll be doing him and me and yourself a great service.'

" 'That I do believe,' says I. 'But sure, you know, Billy, as well as me, having fought against and for us, that the king and me are nothing more than two of the finest men that God Almighty ever made. Nothing more, I do assure you.'

" 'That may be,' says Billy Fish, 'and yet I should be sorry if it was.' He sinks his head upon his great fur cloak for a minute and thinks. 'King,' says he, 'be you man or god or devil, I'll stick by you today. I have twenty of my men with me, and they will follow me. We'll go to Bashkai until the storm blows over.'

"A little snow had fallen in the night, and everything was white except the greasy fat clouds that blew down and down from the north. Dravot came out with his crown on his head, swinging his arms and stamping his feet, and looking more pleased than Punch.

"'For the last time, drop it, Dan,' says I, in a whisper. 'Billy Fish here says that there will be a row.'

"'A row among my people!' says Dravot. 'Not much. Peachey, you're a fool not to get a wife, too. Where's the girl?' says he, with a voice as loud as the braying of a jackass. 'Call up all the chiefs and priests, and let the emperor see if his wife suits him.'

"There was no need to call anyone. They were all there leaning on their guns and spears round the clearing in the center of the pine wood. A deputation of priests went down to the little temple to bring up the girl, and the horns blew up fit to wake the dead. Billy Fish saunters round and gets as close to Daniel as he could, and behind him stood his twenty men with matchlocks. Not a man of them under six feet. I was next to Dravot, and behind me was twenty men of the regular army. Up comes the girl, and a strapping wench she was, covered with silver and turquoises but white as death, and looking back every minute at the priests.

"'She'll do,' said Dan, looking her over.

'What's to be afraid of, lass? Come and kiss me.' He puts his arm round her. She shuts her eyes, gives a bit of a squeak, and down goes her face in the side of Dan's flaming red beard.

"'The slut's bitten me!' says he, clapping his hand to his neck, and, sure enough, his hand was red with blood. Billy Fish and two of his matchlock men catches hold of Dan by the shoulders and drags him into the Bashkai lot, while the priests howl in their lingo, 'Neither god nor devil but a man!' I was all taken aback, for a priest cut at me in front, and the army behind began firing into the Bashkai men.

"'God A-mighty!' says Dan. 'What is the meaning o' this?'

"'Come back! Come away!' says Billy Fish. 'Ruin and mutiny is the matter. We'll break for Bashkai if we can.'

"I tried to give some sort of orders to my men— the men o' the regular army—but it was no use, so I fired into the brown of 'em with an English Martini and drilled three beggars in a line. The valley was full of shouting, howling creatures, and every soul was shrieking. 'Not a god nor a devil but only a man!' The Bashkai troops stuck to Billy Fish all they were worth, but their matchlocks wasn't half as good as the Kabul breechloaders, and four of them dropped. Dan was bellowing like a bull, for he was very wrathy; and Billy Fish had a hard job to prevent him running out at the crowd.

"'We can't stand,' says Billy Fish. 'Make a run for it down the valley! The whole place is against us.' The matchlock men ran, and we went down the valley in spite of Dravot's protestations. He was swearing horribly and crying out that he was a king. The priests rolled great stones on us, and the regular army fired hard, and there wasn't more than six men, not counting Dan, Billy Fish, and Me, that came down to the bottom of the valley alive.

"Then they stopped firing and the horns in the temple blew again. 'Come away—for Gord's sake come away!' says Billy Fish. 'They'll send runners out to all the villages before ever we get to Bashkai. I can protect you there, but I can't do anything now.'

"My own notion is that Dan began to go mad in his head from that hour. He stared up and down like a stuck pig. Then he was all for walking back alone and killing the priests with his bare hands; which he could have done. 'An emperor am I,' says Daniel, 'and next year I shall be a knight of the queen.'

"'All right, Dan,' says I; 'but come along now while there's time.'

"'It's your fault,' says he, 'for not looking after your army better. There was mutiny in the midst, and you didn't know—you damned engine-driving, plate-laying, missionary's pass-hunting hound!' He sat upon a rock and called me every foul name he could lay tongue to. I was too heartsick to care, though it was all his foolishness that brought the smash.

"'I'm sorry, Dan,' says I, 'but there's no accounting for natives. This business is our fifty-seven. Maybe we'll make something out of it yet, when we've got to Bashkai.'

" 'Let's go to Bashkai, then,' says Dan, 'and, by God, when I come back here again I'll sweep the valley so there isn't a bug in a blanket left!'

"We walked all that day, and all that night Dan was stumping up and down on the snow, chewing his beard and muttering to himself.

" 'There's no hope o' getting clear,' said Billy Fish. 'The priests will have sent runners to the villages to say that you are only men. Why didn't you stick on as gods till things was more settled? I'm a dead man,' says Billy Fish, and he throws himself down on the snow and begins to pray to his gods.

"Next morning we was in a cruel bad country —all up and down, no level ground at all, and no food either. The six Bashkai men looked at Billy Fish hungry-wise as if they wanted to ask something, but they said never a word. At noon we came to the top of a flat mountain all covered with snow, and when we climbed up into it, behold, there was an army in position waiting in the middle!

" 'The runners have been very quick,' says Billy Fish, with a little bit of a laugh. 'They are waiting for us.'

"Three or four men began to fire from the enemy's side, and a chance shot took Daniel in the calf of the leg. That brought him to his senses. He looks across the snow at the army, and sees the rifles that we had brought into the country.

" 'We're done for,' says he. 'They are Englishmen, these people, and it's my blasted nonsense that has brought you to this. Get back, Billy Fish, and take your men away; you've done what you could, and now cut for it. Carnehan,' says he, 'shake hands with me and go along with Billy. Maybe they won't kill you. I'll go and meet 'em alone. It's me that did it. Me, the king!'

"'Go!' says I. 'Go to hell, Dan. I'm with you here. Billy Fish, you clear out, and we two will meet those folk.'

"'I'm a chief,' says Billy Fish, quite quiet. 'I stay with you. My men can go.'

"The Bashkai fellows didn't wait for a second word but ran off, and Dan and me and Billy Fish walked across to where the drums were drumming and the horns were horning. It was cold—awful cold. I've got that cold in the back of my head now. There's a lump of it there.''

The punkah coolies had gone to sleep. Two kerosene lamps were blazing in the office, and the perspiration poured down my face and splashed on the blotter as I leaned forward. Carnehan was shivering, and I feared that his mind might go. I wiped my face, took a fresh grip of the piteously mangled hands, and said: ''What happened after that?''

The momentary shift of my eyes had broken the clear current.

''What was you pleased to say?'' whined Carnehan. ''They took them without any sound. Not a little whisper all along the snow, not though the king knocked down the first man that set hand on him—not though old Peachey fired his last cartridge into the brown of 'em. Not a single solitary sound did those swines make. They just closed up tight, and I tell you their furs stunk. There was a man called Billy Fish, a good friend of us all, and they cut his throat, sir, then and there, like a pig; and the king kicks up the bloody snow and says: 'We've had a dashed fine run for our money. What's coming next?' But Peachey, Peachey Taliaferro, I tell you, sir, in confidence as betwixt two friends, he lost his head, sir. No, he didn't neither. The king lost his head, so he did, all along o' one of those cunning rope bridges. Kindly let me have the paper cutter, sir. It tilted this way. They marched him a mile across the snow to a rope bridge over a ravine with a river at the bottom. You may have seen such. They prodded him behind like an ox. 'Damn your eyes!' says the King. 'D'you suppose I can't die like a gentleman?' He turns to Peachey— Peachey that was crying like a child. 'I've brought you to this, Peachey,' says he. 'Brought you out of your happy life to be killed in Kafiristan, where you was late commander-in-chief of the emperor's forces. Say you forgive me, Peachey.' 'I do,' says Peachey. 'Fully and freely do I forgive you, Dan.' 'Shake hands, Peachey,' says he. 'I'm going now.' Out he goes, looking neither right nor left, and when he was plumb in the middle of those dizzy dancing ropes. 'Cut, you beggars,' he shouts; and they cut, and old Dan fell, turning round and round and round twenty thousand miles, for he took half an hour to fall till he struck the water, and I could see his body caught on a rock with the gold crown close beside.

"But do you know what they did to Peachey between two pine trees? They crucified him, sir, as Peachey's hand will show. They used wooden pegs for his hands and his feet; and he didn't die. He hung there and screamed, and they took him down next day, and said it was a miracle that he wasn't dead. They took him down—poor old Peachey that hadn't done them any harm—that hadn't done them any...."

He rocked to and fro and wept bitterly, wiping his eyes with the back of his scarred hands and moaning like a child for some ten minutes.

"They were cruel enough to feed him up in the temple, because they said he was more a god than old Daniel that was a man. Then they turned him out on the snow, and told him to go home, and Peachey came home in about a year, begging along the roads quite safe; for Daniel Dravot he walked before and said: 'Come along, Peachey. It's a big thing we're doing.' The mountains they danced at night, and the mountains they tried to fall on Peachey's head, but Dan he held up his hand, and Peachey came along bent double. He never let go of Dan's hand, and he never let go of Dan's head. They gave it to him as a present in the temple, to remind him not to come again, and though the crown was pure gold, and Peachey was starving, never would Peachey sell the same. You knew Dravot, sir! You knew right worshipful brother Dravot! Look at him now!"

He fumbled in the mass of rags round his bent waist; brought out a black horsehair bag embroidered with silver thread; and shook there-from on to my table—the dried, withered head of Daniel Dravot! The morning sun that had long been paling the lamps struck the red beard and blind sunken eyes; struck, too, a heavy circlet of gold studded with raw turquoises, that Carnehan placed tenderly on the battered temples.

"You behold now," said Carnehan, "the emperor in his habit as he lived—the King of Kafiristan with his crown upon his head. Poor old Daniel that was a monarch once!"

I shuddered, for, in spite of defacements manifold, I recognized the head of the man of Marwar Junction. Carnehan rose to go. I attempted stop him. He was not fit to walk abroad. "Let me take away the whiskey and give me a little money," he gasped. "I was a king once. I'll go to the deputy commissioner and ask to set in the poorhouse till I get my health. No, thank you, I can't wait till you get a carriage for me. I've urgent private affairs—in the south—at Marwar."

He shambled out of the office and departed in the direction of the Deputy Commissioner's house. That day at noon I had occasion to go down the blinding hot mall, and I saw a crooked man crawling along the white dust of the roadside, his hat in his hand, quavering dolorously after the fashion of street singers at home. There was not a soul in sight and he was out of all possible earshot of the houses. And he sang through his nose, turning his head from right to left:

> The Son of Man goes forth to war,
>   A golden crown to gain;
> His blood-red banner streams afar—
>   Who follows in his train?

I waited to hear no more, but put the poor wretch into my carriage and drove him off to the nearest missionary for eventual transfer to the asylum. He repeated the hymn twice while he was with me whom he did not in the least recognize, and I left him singing it to the missionary.

Two days later I inquired after his welfare of the superintendent of the asylum.

"He was admitted suffering from sunstroke. He died early yesterday morning" said the superintendent. "Is it true that he was half an hour bareheaded in the sun at midday?"

"Yes," said I, "but do you happen to know if he had anything upon him by any chance when he died?"

"Not to my knowledge," said the superintendent.

And there the matter rests.

Robert Louis Stevenson

The Sire de Malétroit's Door

Denis de Beaulieu was not yet two-and-twenty, but he counted himself a grown man, and a very accomplished cavalier into the bargain. Lads were early formed in that rough, warfaring epoch; and when one has been in a pitched battle and a dozen raids, has killed one's man in an honorable fashion, and knows a thing or two of strategy and mankind, a certain swagger in the gait is surely to be pardoned. He had put up his horse with due care, and supped with due deliberation; and then, in a very agreeable frame of mind, went out to pay a visit in the gray of the evening. It was not a very wise proceeding on the young man's part. He would have done better to remain beside the fire or go decently to bed. For the town was full of the troops of Burgundy and England under a mixed command; and though Denis was there on safe-conduct, his safe-conduct was like to serve him little on a chance encounter.

It was September 1429; the weather had fallen sharp; a flighty piping wind, laden with showers, beat about the township; and the dead leaves ran riot along the streets. Here and there a window was already lighted up; and the noise of men-at-arms making merry over supper within, came forth in fits and was swallowed up and carried away by the wind. The night fell swiftly; the flag of England, fluttering on the spire top, grew even fainter and fainter against the flying clouds— a black speck like a swallow in the tumultuous, leaden chaos of the sky. As the night fell, the wind rose and began to hoot under archways and roar amid the tree tops in the valley below the town.

Denis de Beaulieu walked fast and was soon knocking at his friend's door; but though he promised himself to stay only a little while and make an early return, his welcome was so pleasant, and he found so much to delay him, that it was already long past midnight before he said goodbye upon the threshold. The wind had fallen again in the meanwhile; the night was as black as the grave; not a star, nor a glimmer of moonshine, slipped through the canopy of cloud. Denis was ill-acquainted with the intricate lanes of Chateau Landon; even by daylight he had found some trouble in picking his way; and in this absolute darkness he soon lost it altogether. He was certain of one thing only—to keep mounting the hill; for his friend's house lay at the lower end, or tail, of Chateau Landon, while the inn was up at the head, under the great church spire. With this clue to go upon he stumbled and groped forward, now breathing more freely in open places where there was a good slice of sky overhead, now feeling along the wall in stifling closes. It is an eerie and mysterious position to be thus submerged in opaque blackness in an almost unknown town. The silence is terrifying in its possibilities. The touch of cold window bars to the exploring hand startles the man like the touch of a toad; the inequalities of the pavement shake his heart into his mouth; a piece of denser darkness threatens an ambuscade or a chasm in the pathway; and where the air is brighter, the houses put on strange and bewildering appearances, as if to lead him farther from his way. For Denis, who had to regain his inn without attracting notice, there was real danger as well as mere discomfort in the walk; and he went warily and boldly at once, and at every corner paused to make an observation.

He had been for some time threading a lane so narrow that he could touch a wall with either hand, when it began to open out and go sharply downward. Plainly this lay no longer in the direction of the inn; but the hope of a little more light tempted him forward to reconnoiter. The lane ended in a terrace with a bartizan wall, which gave an outlook between high houses, as out of an embrasure, into the valley lying dark and formless several hundred feet below. Denis looked down and could discern a few tree tops waving and a single speck of brightness where the river ran across a weir. The weather was clearing up, and the sky had lightened, so as to show the outline of the heavier clouds and the dark margin of the hills. By the uncertain glimmer, the house on his left hand should be a place of some pretensions; it was surmounted by several pinnacles and turret tops; the round stern of a chapel, with a fringe of flying buttresses, projected boldly from the main block; and the door was sheltered under a deep porch carved with figures and overhung by two long gargoyles. The windows of the chapel gleamed through their intricate tracery with a light as of many tapers, and threw out the buttresses and the peaked roof in a more intense blackness against the sky. It was plainly the hotel of some great family of the neighborhood; and as it reminded Denis of a town house of his own at Bourges, he stood for some time gazing up at it and mentally gauging the skill of the architects and the consideration of the two families.

There seemed to be no issue to the terrace but the lane by which he had reached it; he could only retrace his steps, but he had gained some notion of his whereabouts, and hoped by this means to hit the main thoroughfare and speedily regain the inn. He was reckoning without that chapter of accidents which was to make this night memorable above all others in his career; for he had not gone back above a hundred yards before he saw a light coming to meet him, and heard loud voices speaking together in the echoing narrows of the lane. It was a party of men-at-arms going the night-round with torches. Denis assured himself that they had all been making free with the wine bowl, and were in no mood to be particular about safe-conducts or the niceties of chivalrous war. It was as like as not that they would kill him like a

54

dog and leave him where he fell. The situation was inspiriting, but nervous. Their own torches would conceal him from sight, he reflected; and he hoped that they would drown the noise of his footsteps with their own empty voices. If he were but fleet and silent, he might evade their notice altogether.

Unfortunately, as he turned to beat a retreat, his foot rolled upon a pebble; he fell against the wall with an ejaculation, and his sword rang loudly on the stones. Two or three voices demanded who went there—some in French, some in English; but Denis made no reply, and ran the faster down the lane. Once upon the terrace, he paused to look back. They still kept calling after him, and just then began to double the pace in pursuit, with a considerable clank of armor, and great tossing of the torch light to and fro in the narrow jaws of the passage.

Denis cast a look around and darted into the porch. There he might escape observation, or—if that were too much to expect—was in a capital posture whether for parley or defense. So thinking, he drew his sword and tried to set his back against the door. To his surprise, it yielded behind his weight; and though he turned in a moment, continued to swing back on oiled and noiseless hinges, until it stood wide-open on a black interior. When things fall out opportunely for the person concerned, he is not apt to be critical about the how or why, his own immediate personal convenience seeming a sufficient reason for the strangest oddities and revolutions in our sublunary things; and so Denis, without a moment's hesitation, stepped within and partly closed the door behind him to conceal his place of refuge. Nothing was further from his thoughts than to close it altogether; but for some inexplicable reason—perhaps by a spring or a weight —the ponderous mass of oak whipped itself out of his fingers and clanked to, with a formidable rumble and a noise like the falling of an automatic bar.

The round, at that very moment, debouched upon the terrace and proceeded to summon him with shouts and curses. He heard them ferreting in the dark corners, the stock of a lance even rattled along the outer surface of the door behind which he stood; but these gentlemen were in too high a humor to be long delayed, and soon made off down a corkscrew pathway which had escaped Denis's observation, and passed out of sight and hearing along the battlements of the town.

Denis breathed again. He gave them a few minutes' grace for fear of accidents, and then groped about for some means of opening the door and slipping forth again. The inner surface was quite smooth, not a handle, not a molding, not a projection of any sort. He got his fingernails round the edges and pulled, but the mass was immovable. He shook it; it was as firm as a rock. Denis de Beaulieu frowned and gave vent to a little noiseless whistle. What ailed the door? he wondered. Why was it open? How came it to shut so easily and so effectually after him? There was something obscure and underhand about all this that was little to the young man's fancy. It looked like a snare; and yet who would suppose a snare in such a quiet bystreet and in a house of so prosperous and even noble an exterior? And yet—snare or no snare, intentionally or unintentionally—here he was, prettily trapped; and for the life of him he could see no way out of it again. The darkness began to weigh upon him. He gave ear; all was silent without, but within and close by he seemed to catch a faint sighing, a faint sobbing rustle, a little stealthy creak—as though many persons were at his side, holding themselves quite still, and governing even their respiration with the extreme of slyness. The idea went to his vitals with a shock, and he faced about suddenly as if to defend his life. Then, for the first time, he became aware of a light about the level of his eyes and at some distance in the interior of the house—a vertical thread of light, widening towards the bottom, such as might escape between two wings of arras over a doorway. To see anything was a relief to Denis; it was like a piece of solid ground to a man laboring in a morass; his mind seized upon it with avidity; and he stood staring at it and trying to piece together some logical conception of his surroundings. Plainly there was a flight of steps ascending from his own level to that of this illuminated doorway; and indeed he thought he could make out another thread of light, as fine as a needle, and as faint as phosphorescence, which might very well be reflected along the polished wood of a handrail. Since he had begun to suspect that he was not alone, his heart had continued to beat with smothering violence, and an intolerable desire for action of any sort had possessed itself of his spirit. He was in deadly peril, he believed.

What could be more natural than to mount the staircase, lift the curtain, and confront his difficulty at once? At least he would be dealing with something tangible; at least he would be no longer in the dark. He stepped slowly forward with outstretched hand, until his foot struck the bottom step; then he rapidly scaled the stairs, stood for a moment to compose his expression, lifted the arras, and went in.

He found himself in a large apartment of polished stone. There were three doors; one on each of three sides; all similarly curtained with tapestry. The fourth side was occupied by two large windows and a great stone chimney piece, carved with the arms of the Malétroits. Denis recognized the bearings, and was gratified to find himself in such good hands. The room was strongly illuminated; but it contained little furniture except a heavy table and a chair or two, the hearth was innocent of fire, and the pavement was but sparsely strewn with rushes clearly many days old.

On a high chair beside the chimney, and directly facing Denis as he entered, sat a little old gentleman in a fur tippet. He sat with his legs crossed and his hands folded, and a cup of spiced wine stood by his elbow on a bracket on the wall. His countenance had a strongly masculine cast; not properly human, but such as we see in the bull, the goat, or the domestic boar; something equivocal and wheedling, something greedy, brutal, and dangerous. The upper lip was inordinately full, as though swollen by a blow or a toothache; and the smile, the peaked eyebrows, and the small, strong eyes were quaintly and almost comically evil in expression. Beautiful white hair hung straight all round his head, like a saint's, and fell in a single curl upon the tippet. His beard and mustache were the pink of venerable sweetness. Age, probably in consequence of inordinate precautions, had left no mark upon his hands; and the Malétroit hand was famous. It would be difficult to imagine anything at once so fleshy and so delicate in design; the tapered, sensual fingers were like those of one of Leonardo's women; the fork of the thumb made a dimpled protuberance when closed; the nails were perfectly shaped, and of a dead, surprising whiteness. It rendered his aspect tenfold more redoubtable, that a man with hands like these should keep them devoutly folded in his lap like a virgin martyr—that a man with so intense and startling an expression of face should sit patiently on his seat and contemplate people with an unwinking stare, like a god, or a god's statue. His quiescence seemed ironical and treacherous, it fitted so poorly with his looks.

Such was Alain, Sire de Malétroit.

Denis and he looked silently at each other for a second or two.

"Pray step in," said the Sire de Malétroit. "I have been expecting you all the evening."

He had not arisen, but he accompanied his words with a smile and a slight but courteous inclination of the head. Partly from the smile, partly from the strange musical murmur with which the Sire prefaced his observation, Denis felt a strong shudder of disgust go through his marrow. And what with disgust and honest confusion of mind, he could scarcely get words together in reply.

"I fear," he said, "that this is a double accident. I am not the person you suppose me. It seems you were looking for a visit; but for my part, nothing was further from my thoughts—nothing could be more contrary to my wishes—than this intrusion."

"Well, well," replied the old gentleman indulgently, "here you are, which is the main point. Seat yourself, my friend, and put yourself entirely at your ease. We shall arrange our little affairs presently."

Denis perceived that the matter was still complicated with some misconception, and he hastened to continue his explanation.

"Your door..." he began.

"About my door?" asked the other, raising his peaked eyebrows. "A little piece of ingenuity." And he shrugged his shoulders. "A hospitable fancy! By your own account, you were not desirous of making my acquaintance. We old people look for such reluctance now and then; and when it touches our honor, we cast about until we find some way of overcoming it. You arrive uninvited, but believe me, very welcome."

"You persist in error, sir," said Denis. "There can be no question between you and me. I am a stranger in this countryside. My name is Denis, damoiseau de Beaulieu. If you see me in your house, it is only—"

"My young friend," interrupted the other, "you will permit me to have my own ideas on that subject. They probably differ from yours at the present moment," he added, with a leer, "but time will show which of us is in the right."

Denis was convinced he had to do with a lunatic. He seated himself with a shrug, content to wait the upshot; and a pause ensued, during which he thought he could distinguish a hurried gabbling as of prayer from behind the arras immediately opposite him. Sometimes there seemed to be but one person engaged, sometimes two; and the vehemence of the voice, low as it was, seemed to indicate either great haste or an agony of spirit. It occurred to him that this piece of tapestry covered the entrance to the chapel he had noticed from without.

The old gentleman meanwhile surveyed Denis from head to foot with a smile, and from time to time emitted little noises like a bird or a mouse, which seemed to indicate a high degree of satisfaction. This state of matters became rapidly insupportable; and Denis to put an end to it, remarked politely that the wind had gone down.

The old gentleman fell into a fit of silent laughter, so prolonged and violent that he became quite red in the face. Denis got upon his feet at once, and put on his hat with a flourish.

"Sir," he said, "if you are in your wits, you have affronted me grossly. If you are out of them, I flatter myself I can find better employment for my brains than to talk with lunatics. My conscience is clear; you have made a fool of me from the first moment; you have refused to hear my explanations; and now there is no power under God will make me stay here any longer;

and if I cannot make my way out in a more decent fashion, I will hack your door in pieces with my sword."

The Sire de Malêtroit raised his right hand and wagged it at Denis with the fore and little fingers extended.

"My dear nephew," he said, "sit down."

"Nephew!" retorted Denis. "You lie in your throat"; and he snapped his fingers in his face.

"Sit down, you rogue!" cried the old gentleman, in a sudden harsh voice, like the barking of a dog. "Do you fancy," he went on, "that when I had made my little contrivance for the door I had stopped short with that? If you prefer to be bound hand and foot till your bones ache, rise and try to go away. If you choose to remain a free young buck, agreeably conversing with an old gentleman—why, sit where you are in peace, and God be with you."

"Do you mean I am a prisoner?" demanded Denis.

"I state the facts," replied the other. "I would rather leave the conclusion to yourself."

Denis sat down again. Externally he managed to keep pretty calm; but within, he was now boiling with anger, now chilled with apprehension. He no longer felt convinced that he was dealing with a madman. And if the old gentleman was sane, what, in God's name, had he to look for? What absurd or tragical adventure had befallen him? What countenance was he to assume?

While he was thus unpleasantly reflecting, the arras that overhung the chapel door was raised, and a tall priest in his robes came forth and, giving a long, keen stare at Denis, said something in an undertone to the Sire de Malétroit.

"She is in a better frame of spirit?" asked the latter.

"She is more resigned, messire," replied the priest.

"Now the Lord help her, she is hard to please!" sneered the old gentleman. "A likely stripling— not ill-born—and of her own choosing, too? Why, what more would the jade have?"

"The situation is not usual for a young damsel," said the other, "and somewhat trying to her blushes."

"She should have thought of that before she began the dance. It was none of my choosing, God knows that: but since she is in it, by our Lady, she shall carry it to the end." And then addressing Denis, "Monsieur de Beaulieu," he asked, "may I present you to my niece? She has been waiting your arrival, I may say, with even greater impatience than myself."

Denis had resigned himself with a good grace— all he desired was to know the worst of it as speedily as possible; so he rose at once, and bowed in acquiescence. The Sire de Malétroit followed his example and limped, with the assistance of the chaplain's arm, towards the chapel door. The priest pulled aside the arras, and all three entered. The building had considerable architectural pretensions. A light groining sprang from six stout columns, and hung down in two rich pendants from the center of the vault. The place terminated behind the altar in a round end, embossed and honeycombed with a superfluity of ornament in relief, and pierced by many little windows shaped like stars, trefoils, or wheels. These windows were imperfectly glazed, so that the night air circulated freely in the chapel. The tapers, of which there must have been half a hundred burning on the altar, were unmercifully blown about; and the light went through many different phases of brilliancy and semieclipse. On the steps in front of the altar knelt a young girl richly attired as a bride. A chill settled over Denis as he observed her costume; he fought with desperate energy against the conclusion that was thrust upon his mind; it could not—it should not—be as he feared.

"Blanche," said the Sire, in his most flutelike tones, "I have brought a friend to see you, my little girl; turn round and give him your pretty hand. It is good to be devout; but it is necessary to be polite, my niece."

The girl rose to her feet and turned towards the newcomers. She moved all of a piece; and shame and exhaustion were expressed in every line of her fresh young body; and she held her head down and kept her eyes upon the pavement, as she came slowly forward. In the course of her advance, her eyes fell upon Denis de Beaulieu's feet—of which he was justly vain, be it remarked, and wore in the most elegant accouterment even while traveling. She paused —started, as if his yellow boots had conveyed some shocking meaning—and glanced suddenly up into the wearer's countenance. Their eyes met; shame gave place to horror and terror in her looks; the blood left her lips; with a piercing scream she covered her face with her hands and sank upon the chapel floor.

"That is not the man!" she cried. "My uncle, that is not the man!"

The Sire de Malétroit chirped agreeably. "Of course not," he said; "I expected as much. It was so unfortunate you could not remember his name."

"Indeed," she cried, "indeed, I have never seen this person till this moment—I have never so much as set eyes upon him—I never wish to see him again. Sir," she said, turning to Denis, "if you are a gentleman, you will bear me out. Have I ever seen you—have you ever seen me—before this accursed hour!"

"To speak for myself, I have never had that pleasure," answered the young man. "This is the first time, messire, that I have met with your engaging niece."

The old gentleman shrugged his shoulders.

"I am distressed to hear it," he said. "But it is never too late to begin. I had little more acquaintance with my own late lady ere I married her; which proves," he added with a grimace, "that these impromptu marriages may often produce an excellent understanding in the long run. As the bridegroom is to have a voice in the matter, I will give him two hours to make up for lost time before we proceed with the ceremony." And he turned towards the door, followed by the clergyman.

The girl was on her feet in a moment. "My uncle, you cannot be in earnest," she said. "I declare before God I will stab myself rather than be forced on that young man. The heart rises at it; God forbids such marriages; you dishonor your white hair. Oh, my uncle, pity me! There is not a woman in all the world but would prefer death to such a nuptial. Is it possible," she added, faltering, "is it possible that you do not believe me—that you still think this"—and she pointed at Denis with a tremor of anger and contempt—"that you still think *this* to be the man?"

"Frankly," said the old gentleman, pausing on the threshold, "I do. But let me explain to you once for all, Blanche de Malétroit, my way of thinking about this affair. When you took it into your head to dishonor my family and the name that I have borne, in peace and war, for more than three-score years, you forfeited, not only the right to question my designs, but that of looking me in the face. If your father had been alive, he would have spat on you and turned you out-of-doors. His was the hand of iron. You may bless your God you have only to deal with the hand of velvet, mademoiselle. It was my duty to get you married without delay. Out of pure good will, I have tried to find your own gallant for you. And I believe I have succeeded. But before God and all the holy angels, Blanche de Malétroit, if I have not, I care not one jackstraw. So let me recommend you to be polite to our young friend; for upon my word, your next groom may be less appetizing."

And with that he went out, with the chaplain at his heels; and the arras fell behind the pair.

The girl turned upon Denis with flashing eyes.

"And what, sir," she demanded, "may be the meaning of all this?"

"God knows," returned Denis gloomily. "I am a prisoner in this house, which seems full of mad people. More I know not, and nothing do I understand."

"And how came you here?" she asked.

He told her as briefly as he could. "For the rest," he added, "perhaps you will follow my example, and tell me the answer to all these riddles, and what, in God's name, is like to be the end of it."

She stood silent for a little, and he could see her lips tremble and her tearless eyes burn with a feverish luster. Then she pressed her forehead in both hands.

"Alas, how my head aches!" she said wearily —"to say nothing of my poor heart! But it is due to you to know my story, unmaidenly as it must seem. I am called Blanche de Malétroit; I have been without father or mother for—oh! for as long as I can recollect, and indeed I have been most unhappy all my life. Three months ago a young captain began to stand near me every day in church. I could see that I pleased him; I am much to blame, but I was so glad that anyone should love me; and when he passed me a letter, I took it home with me and read it with great pleasure. Since that time he has written many. He was so anxious to speak with me, poor fellow! and kept asking me to leave the door open some evening that we might have two words upon the stair. For he knew how much my uncle trusted me." She gave something

67

like a sob at that, and it was a moment before she could go on. "My uncle is a hard man, but he is very shrewd," she said at last. "He has performed many feats in war, and was a great person at court, and much trusted by Queen Isabeau in old days. How he came to suspect me I cannot tell; but it is hard to keep anything from his knowledge; and this morning, as we came from mass, he took my hand in his, forced it open, and read my little billet, walking by my side all the while. When he had finished, he gave it back to me with great politeness. It contained another request to have the door left open; and this has been the ruin of us all. My uncle kept me strictly in my room until evening, and then ordered me to dress myself as you see me—a hard mockery for a young girl, do you not think so? I suppose, when he could not prevail with me to tell him the young captain's name, he must have laid a trap for him: into which you have fallen in the anger of God. I looked for much confusion; for how could I tell whether he was willing to take me for his wife on these sharp terms? He might have been trifling with me from the first; or I might have made myself too cheap in his eyes. But truly I had not looked for such a shameful punishment as this! I could not think that God would let a girl be so disgraced before a young man. And now I have told you all; and I can scarcely hope that you will not despise me."

Denis made her a respectful inclination.

"Madam," he said, "you have honored me by your confidence. It remains for me to prove that I am not unworthy of the honor. Is Messire de Malétroit at hand?"

"I believe he is writing in the salle without," she answered.

"May I lead you thither, madam?" asked Denis, offering his hand with his most courtly bearing.

She accepted it; and the pair passed out of the chapel, Blanche in a very drooping and shame-faced condition, but Denis strutting and ruffling in the consciousness of a mission, and the boyish certainty of accomplishing it with honor.

The Sire de Malētroit rose to meet them with an ironical obeisance.

"Sir," said Denis, with the grandest possible air, "I believe I am to have some say in the matter of this marriage; and let me tell you at once, I will be no party to forcing the inclination of this young lady. Had it been freely offered to me, I should have been proud to accept her hand, for I perceive she is as good as she is beautiful; but as things are, I have now the honor, messire, of refusing."

Blanche looked at him with gratitude in her eyes; but the old gentleman only smiled and smiled, until his smile grew positively sickening to Denis.

"I am afraid," he said, "Monsieur de Beaulieu, that you do not perfectly understand the choice I have to offer you. Follow me, I beseech you, to this window." And he led the way to one of the large windows which stood open on the night. "You observe," he went on, "there is an iron ring in the upper masonry, and reeved through that a very efficacious rope. Now, mark my words; if you should find your disinclination to my niece's person insurmountable, I shall have you hanged out of this window before sunrise. I shall proceed to such an extremity with the greatest regret, you may believe me. For it is not at all your death that I desire, but my niece's establishment in life. At the same time, it must come to that if you prove obstinate. Your family, Monsieur de Beaulieu, is very well in its way; but if you sprang from Charlemagne, you should not refuse the hand of a Malétroit with impunity—not if she had been as common as the Paris road—not if she were as hideous as the gargoyle over my door. Neither my niece nor you, nor my own private feelings, move me at all in this matter. The honor of my house has been compromised; I believe you to be the guilty person; at least you are now in the secret; and you can hardly wonder if I request you to wipe out the stain. If you will not, your blood be on your own head! It will be no great satisfaction to me to have your interesting relics kicking their heels in the breeze below my windows; but half a loaf is better than no bread, and if I cannot cure the dishonor, I shall at least stop the scandal.''

There was a pause.

''I believe there are other ways of settling such imbroglios among gentlemen,'' said Denis. ''You wear a sword, and I hear you have used it with distinction.''

The Sire de Malétroit made a signal to the chaplain, who crossed the room with long silent strides and raised the arras over the third of the three doors. It was only a moment before he let it fall again; but Denis had time to see a dusky passage full of armed men.

''When I was a little younger, I should have

been delighted to honor you, Monsieur de Beaulieu," said Sire Alain; "but I am now too old. Faithful retainers are the sinews of age, and I must employ the strength I have. This is one of the hardest things to swallow as a man grows up in years; but with a little patience, even this becomes habitual. You and the lady seem to prefer the salle for what remains of your two hours; and as I have no desire to cross your preference, I shall resign it to your use with all the pleasure in the world. No haste!" he added, holding up his hand, as he saw a dangerous look come into Denis de Beaulieu's face. "If your mind revolts against hanging, it will be time enough two hours hence to throw yourself out of the window or upon the pikes of my retainers. Two hours of life are always two hours. A great many things may turn up in even as little a while as that. And, besides, if I understand her appearance, my niece has still something to say to you. You will not disfigure your last hours by a want of politeness to a lady?"

Denis looked at Blanche, and she made him an imploring gesture.

It is likely that the old gentleman was hugely pleased at this symptom of an understanding; for he smiled on both, and added sweetly: "If you will give me your word of honor, Monsieur de Beaulieu, to await my return at the end of the two hours before attempting anything desperate, I shall withdraw my retainers, and let you speak in greater privacy with mademoiselle."

Denis again glanced at the girl, who seemed to beseech him to agree.

"I give you my word of honor," he said.

Messire de Malétroit bowed, and proceeded to limp about the apartment, clearing his throat the while with that odd musical chirp which had already grown so irritating in the ears of Denis de Beaulieu. He first possessed himself of some papers which lay upon the table; then he went to the mouth of the passage and appeared to give an order to the men behind the arras; and lastly he hobbled out through the door by which Denis had come in, turning upon the threshold to address a last smiling bow to the young couple, and followed by the chaplain with a hand lamp.

No sooner were they alone than Blanche advanced toward Denis with her hands extended. Her face was flushed and excited, and her eyes shone with tears.

"You shall not die!" she cried. "You shall marry me after all."

"You seem to think, madam," replied Denis, "that I stand much in fear of death."

"Oh, no, no," she said. "I see you are no poltroon. It is for my own sake—I could not bear to have you slain for such a scruple."

"I am afraid," returned Denis, "that you underrate the difficulty, madam. What you may be too generous to refuse, I may be too proud to accept. In a moment of noble feeling towards me, you forget what you perhaps owe to others."

He had the decency to keep his eyes upon the floor as he said this, and after he had finished, so as not to spy upon her confusion. She stood silent for a moment, then walked suddenly away, and falling on her uncle's chair, fairly burst out sobbing. Denis was in the acme of embarrassment. He looked round, as if to seek for inspiration, and seeing a stool, plumped down upon it for something to do. There he sat, playing with the guard of his rapier, and wishing himself dead a thousand times over, and buried in the nastiest kitchen heap in France. His eyes wandered round the apartment, but found nothing to arrest them. There were such wide spaces between the furniture, the light fell so badly and cheerlessly over all, the dark outside air looked in so coldly through the windows, that he thought he had never seen a church so vast, nor a tomb so melancholy. The regular sobs of Blanche de Malétroit measured out the time like the ticking of a clock. He read the device upon the shield over and over again, until his eyes became obscured; he stared into shadowy corners until he imagined they were swarming with horrible animals; and every now and again he awoke with a start, to remember that his last two hours were running, and death was on the march.

Oftener and oftener, as the time went on, did his glance settle on the girl herself. Her face was bowed forward and covered with her hands, and she was shaken at intervals by the convulsive hiccup of grief. Even thus she was not an unpleasant object to dwell upon, so plump and yet so fine, with a warm brown skin, and the most beautiful hair, Denis thought, in the whole world of womankind. Her hands were like her uncle's; but they were more in place at the end of her young arms, and looked infinitely soft and caressing. He remembered how her blue eyes had shone upon him, full of anger, pity, and innocence. And the more he dwelt on her perfections, the uglier death looked, and the more deeply was he smitten with penitence at her continued tears. Now he felt that no man could have the courage to leave a world which contained so beautiful a creature; and now he would have given forty minutes of his last hour to have unsaid his cruel speech.

Suddenly a hoarse and ragged peal of cockcrow rose to their ears from the dark valley below the windows, and this shattering noise in the silence of all around was like a light in a dark place, and shook them both out of their reflections.

"Alas, can I do nothing to help you?" she said, looking up.

"Madam," replied Denis, with a fine irrelevancy, "if I have said anything to wound you, believe me, it was for your own sake and not for mine."

She thanked him with a tearful look.

"I feel your position cruelly," he went on. "The world has been bitter hard on you. Your uncle is a disgrace to mankind. Believe me, madam, there is no young gentleman in all France but would be glad of my opportunity to die in doing you a momentary service."

"I know already that you can be very brave and generous," she answered. "What I *want* to know is whether I can serve you—now or afterwards," she added, with a quaver.

"Most certainly," he answered, with a smile. "Let me sit beside you as if I were a friend, instead of a foolish intruder; try to forget how awkwardly we are placed to one another; make my last moments go pleasantly; and you will do me the chief service possible."

74

"You are very gallant," she added, with a yet deeper sadness..."very gallant...and it somehow pains me. But draw nearer, if you please; and if you find anything to say to me, you will at least make certain of a very friendly listener. Ah! Monsieur de Beaulieu," she broke forth—"ah! Monsieur de Beaulieu, how can I look you in the face?" And she fell to weeping again with a renewed effusion.

"Madam," said Denis, taking her hand in both of his, "reflect on the little time I have before me, and the great bitterness into which I am cast by the sight of your distress. Spare me, in my last moments, the spectacle of what I cannot cure even with the sacrifice of my life."

"I am very selfish," answered Blanche. "I will be braver, Monsieur de Beaulieu, for your sake. But think if I can do you no kindness in the future—if you have no friends to whom I could carry your adieus. Charge me as heavily as you can; every burden will lighten, by so little, the invaluable gratitude I owe you. Put it in my power to do something more for you than weep."

"My mother is married again, and has a young family to care for. My brother Guichard will inherit my fiefs; and if I am not in error, that will content him amply for my death. Life is a little vapor that passeth away, as we are told by those in holy orders. When a man is in a fair way and sees all life open in front of him, he seems to himself to make a very important figure in the world. His horse whinnies to him; the trumpets blow and the girls look out of windows as he rides into town before his company; he receives many assurances

75

of trust and regard—sometimes by express in a letter —sometimes face to face, with persons of great consequence falling on his neck. It is not wonderful if his head is turned for a time. But once he is dead, were he as brave as Hercules or as wise as Solomon, he is soon forgotten. It is not ten years since my father fell, with many other knights around him, in a very fierce encounter, and I do not think that anyone of them, nor so much as the name of the fight, is now remembered. No, no, madam, the nearer you come to it, you see that death is a dark and dusty corner, where a man gets into his tomb and has the door shut after him till the Judgment Day. I have few friends just now, and once I am dead I shall have none."

"Ah, Monsieur de Beaulieu!" she exclaimed. "You forget Blanche de Malétroit."

"You have a sweet nature, madam, and you are pleased to estimate a little service far beyond its worth."

"It is not that," she answered. "You mistake me if you think I am so easily touched by my own concerns. I say so, because you are the noblest man I have ever met; because I recognize in you a spirit that would have made even a common person famous in the land."

"And yet here I die in a mousetrap—with no more noise about it than my own speaking," answered he.

A look of pain crossed her face, and she was silent for a little while. Then a light came into her eyes, and with a smile she spoke again.

"I cannot have my champion think meanly of himself. Anyone who gives his life for another will be met in Paradise by all the heralds and angels of the Lord God. And you have no such cause to hang your head. For...pray, do you think me beautiful?'' she asked, with a deep flush.

''Indeed, madam, I do,'' he said.

''I am glad of that,'' she answered heartily. ''Do you think there are many men in France who have been asked in marriage by a beautiful maiden—with her own lips—and who have refused her to her face? I know you men would half despise such a triumph; but, believe me, we women know more of what is precious in love. There is nothing that should set a person higher in his own esteem; and we women would prize nothing more dearly.''

''You are very good,'' he said; ''but you cannot make me forget that I was asked in pity and not for love.''

''I am not so sure of that,'' she replied, holding down her head. ''Hear me to an end, Monsieur de Beaulieu. I know how you must despise me; I feel you are right to do so; I am too poor a creature to occupy one thought of your mind, although, alas! you must die for me this morning. But when I asked you to marry me, indeed, and indeed, it was because I respected and admired you, and loved you with my whole soul, from the very moment that you took my part against my uncle. If you had seen yourself, and how noble you looked, you would pity rather than despise me. And now,'' she went on, hurriedly checking him with her hand, ''although I have laid aside all reserve and told you so much, remember that I know your sentiments towards me already. I would not, believe me, being nobly born, weary you with importunities into consent. I too have a pride of my own: and I declare before the holy mother of God, if you should now go back from your word already given, I would no more marry you than I would marry my uncle's groom."

Denis smiled a little bitterly.

"It is a small love," he said, "that shies at a little pride."

She made no answer, although she probably had her own thoughts.

"Come hither to the window," he said, with a sigh. "Here is the dawn."

And indeed the dawn was already beginning. The hollow of the sky was full of essential daylight, colorless and clean; and the valley underneath was flooded with a gray reflection. A few thin vapors clung in the coves of the forest or lay along the winding course of the river. The scene disengaged a surprising effect of stillness, which was hardly interrupted when the cocks began once more to crow among the steadings. Perhaps the same fellow who had made so horrid a clangor in the darkness not half an hour before, now sent up the merriest cheer to greet the coming day. A little wind went bustling and eddying among the tree tops underneath the windows. And still the daylight kept flooding insensibly out of the east, which was soon to grow incandescent and cast up that red-hot cannonball, the rising sun.

Denis looked out over all this with a bit of a shiver. He had taken her hand and retained it in his almost unconsciously.

"Has the day begun already?" she said; and

then, illogically enough: "the night has been so long! Alas! What shall we say to my uncle when he returns?"

"What you will," said Denis, and he pressed her fingers in his.

She was silent.

"Blanche," he said, with a swift, uncertain, passionate utterance, "you have seen whether I fear death. You must know well enough that I would as gladly leap out of that window into the empty air as lay a finger on you without your free and full consent. But if you care for me at all do not let me lose my life in a misapprehension; for I love you better than the whole world; and though I will die for you blithely, it would be like all the joys of Paradise to live on and spend my life in your service."

As he stopped speaking, a bell began to ring loudly in the interior of the house; and a clatter of armor in the corridor showed that the retainers were returning to their post, and the two hours were at an end.

"After all that you have heard?" she whispered, leaning towards him with her lips and eyes.

"I have heard nothing," he replied.

"The captain's name was Fiorimond de Champdivers," she said in his ear.

"I did not hear it," he answered, taking her supple body in his arms and covering her wet face with kisses.

A melodious chirping was audible behind, followed by a beautiful chuckle, and the voice of Messire de Malétroit wished his new nephew a good morning.

Arthur Conan Doyle

How the Brigadier Saved an Army

I have told you, my friends, how we held the
English shut up for six months, from October
1810, to March 1811, within their lines of Torres
Vedras. It was during this time that I hunted the
fox in their company, and showed them that
amidst all their sportsmen there was not one who
could outride a Hussar of Conflans. When I gal-
loped back into the French lines with the blood of
the creature still moist upon my blade, the
outposts who had seen what I had done raised a
frenzied cry in my honor, whilst these English
hunters still yelled behind me, so that I had the
applause of both armies. It made the tears rise to
my eyes to feel that I had won the admiration of so
many brave men. These English are generous
foes. That very evening there came a packet
under a white flag addressed, "To the Hussar
officer who cut down the fox." Within I found the
fox itself in two pieces, as I had left it. There was a

note also, short, but hearty as the English fashion is, to say that as I had slaughtered the fox it only remained for me to eat it. They could not know that it was not our French custom to eat foxes, and it showed their desire that he who had won the honors of the chase should also partake of the game. It is not for a Frenchman to be outdone in politeness, and so I returned it to these brave hunters, and begged them to accept it as a side dish for their next *dejeuner de la chasse*. It is thus that chivalrous opponents make war.

I had brought back with me from my ride a clear plan of the English lines, and this I laid before Massena that very evening.

I had hoped that it would lead him to attack, but all the marshals were at each other's throats, snapping and growling like so many hungry hounds. Ney hated Massena, and Massena hated Junot, and Soult hated them all. For this reason nothing was done. In the meantime food grew more and more scarce, and our beautiful cavalry was ruined for want of fodder. With the end of the winter we had swept the whole country bare, and nothing remained for us to eat, although we sent our forage parties far and wide. It was clear even to the bravest of us that the time had come to retreat. I was myself forced to admit it.

But retreat was not so easy. Not only were the troops weak and exhausted from want of supplies, but the enemy had been much encouraged by our long inaction. Of Wellington we had no great fear. We had found him to be brave and cautious, but with little enterprise. Besides, in that barren country his pursuit could not be rapid. But on our flanks and in our rear there had gathered great numbers of Portuguese militia, of armed peasants, and of guerillas. These people had kept a safe distance all the winter but now that our horses were foundered they were as thick as flies all round our outposts, and no man's life was worth a sou when once he fell into their hands. I could name a dozen officers of my own acquaintance who were cut off during that time, and the luckiest was he who received a ball from behind a rock through his head or his heart. There were some whose deaths were so terrible that no report of them was ever allowed to reach their relatives. So frequent were these tragedies, and so much did they impress the imagination of the men, that it became very difficult to induce them to leave the camp. There was one especial scoundrel, a guerilla chief named Manuelo, "The Smiler," whose exploits filled our men with horror. He was a large, fat man of jovial aspect, and he lurked with a fierce gang among the mountains which lay upon our left flank. A volume might be written of this fellow's cruelties and brutalities, but he was certainly a man of power, for he organized his brigands in a manner which made it almost impossible for us to get through his country. This he did by imposing a severe discipline upon them and enforcing it by cruel penalties, a policy by which he made them formidable, but which had some unexpected results, as I will show you in my story. Had he not flogged his own lieutenant—but you will hear of that when the time comes.

There were many difficulties in connection

with a retreat, but it was very evident that there was no other possible course, and so Massena began to quickly pass his baggage and his sick from Torres Novas, which was his headquarters, to Coimbra, the first strong post on his line of communications. He could not do this unperceived, however, and at once the guerillas came swarming closer and closer upon our flanks. One of our divisions, that of Clausel, with a brigade of Montbrun's cavalry, was far to the south of the Tagus, and it became very necessary to let them know that we were about to retreat, for otherwise they would be left unsupported in the very heart of the enemy's country. I remember wondering how Massena would accomplish this, for simple couriers could not get through, and small parties would be certainly destroyed. In some way an order to fall back must be conveyed to these men, or France would be the weaker by fourteen thousand men. Little did I think that it was I, Colonel Gerard, who was to have the honor of a deed which might have formed the crowning glory of any other man's life, and which stands high among those exploits which have made my own so famous.

At that time I was serving on Massena's staff, and he had two other aides-de-camp, who were also very brave and intelligent officers. The name of one was Cortex and of the other Duplessis. They were senior to me in age, but junior in every other respect. Cortex was a small, dark man, very quick and eager. He was a fine soldier, but he was ruined by his conceit. To take him at his own valuation, he was the first man in the army.

Duplessis was a Gascon, like myself, and he was a very fine fellow, as all Gascon gentlemen are. We took it in turn, day about, to do duty, and it was Cortex who was in attendance upon the morning of which I speak. I saw him at breakfast, but afterwards neither he nor his horse was to be seen. All day Massena was in his usual gloom, and he spent much of his time staring with his telescope at the English lines and at the shipping in the Tagus. He said nothing of the mission upon which he had sent our comrade, and it was not for us to ask him any questions.

That night, about twelve o'clock, I was standing outside the Marshal's headquarters when he came out and stood motionless for half an hour, his arms folded upon his breast, staring through the darkness towards the east. So rigid and intent was he that you might have believed the muffled figure and the cocked hat to have been the statue of the man. What he was looking for I could not imagine; but at last he gave a bitter curse, and, turning on his heel, he went back into the house, banging the door behind him.

Next day the second aide-de-camp, Duplessis, had an interview with Massena in the morning, after which neither he nor his horse was seen again. That night, as I sat in the anteroom, the Marshal passed me, and I observed him through the window standing and staring to the east exactly as he had done before. For fully half an hour he remained there, a black shadow in the gloom. Then he strode in, the door banged, and I heard his spurs and his scabbard jingling and clanking through the passage. At the best he was a savage old man, but when he was crossed I had almost as soon face the Emperor himself. I heard him that night cursing and stamping above my head, but he did not send for me, and I knew him too well to go unsought.

Next morning it was my turn, for I was the only aide-de-camp left. I was his favorite aide-de-camp. His heart went out always to a smart soldier. I declare that I think there were tears in his black eyes when he sent for me that morning.

"Gerard!" said he. "Come here!"

With a friendly gesture he took me by the sleeve and he led me to the open window which faced the east. Beneath us was the infantry camp, and beyond that the lines of the cavalry with the long rows of picketed horses. We could see the French outposts, and then a stretch of open country, intersected by vineyards. A range of hills lay beyond, with one well-marked peak towering above them. Round the base of these hills was a broad belt of forest. A single road ran white and clear, dipping and rising until it passed through a gap in the hills.

"This," said Massena, pointing to the mountain, "is the Sierra de Merodal. Do you perceive anything upon the top?"

I answered that I did not.

"Now?" he asked, and he handed me his field glass.

"What you see," said the Marshal, "is a pile of logs which was placed there as a beacon. We laid it when the country was in our hands, and now, although we no longer hold it, the beacon remains undisturbed. Gerard, that beacon must be lit tonight. France needs it, the Emperor needs it, the army needs it. Two of your comrades have gone to light it, but neither has made his way to the summit. Today it is your turn, and I pray that you may have better luck.''

It is not for a soldier to ask the reason for his orders, and so I was about to hurry from the room, but the Marshal laid his hand upon my shoulder and held me.

"You shall know all, and so learn how high is the cause for which you risk your life,'' said he. "Fifty miles to the south of us, on the other side of the Tagus, is the army of General Clausel. His camp is situated near a peak named the Sierra d'Ossa. On the summit of this peak is a beacon, and by this beacon he has a picket. It is agreed between us that when at midnight he shall see our signal fire he shall light his own as an answer, and shall then at once fall back upon the main army. If he does not start at once I must go without him. For two days I have endeavored to send him his message. It must reach him today, or his army will be left behind and destroyed.''

Ah, my friends, how my heart swelled when I heard how high was the task which fortune had assigned to me! If my life were spared, here was one more splendid new leaf for my laurel crown. If, on the other hand, I died, then it would be a death worthy of such a career. I said nothing, but I cannot doubt that all the noble thoughts that were in me shone in my face, for Massena took my hand and wrung it.

"There is the hill and there the beacon,'' said he. "There is only this guerilla and his men between you and it. I cannot detach a large party for the enterprise, and a small one would be seen and destroyed. Therefore to you alone I commit it. Carry it out in your own way, but at twelve o'clock this night let me see the fire upon the hill."

"If it is not there," said I, "then I pray you, Marshal Massena, to see that my effects are sold and the money sent to my mother." So I raised my hand to my busby and turned upon my heel, my heart glowing at the thought of the great exploit which lay before me.

I sat in my own chamber for some little time considering how I had best take the matter in hand. The fact that neither Cortex nor Duplessis, who were very zealous and active officers, had succeeded in reaching the summit of the Sierra de Merodal showed that the country was very closely watched by the guerillas. I reckoned out the distance upon a map. There were ten miles of open country to be crossed before reaching the hills. Then came a belt of forest on the lower slopes of the mountain, which may have been three or four miles wide. And then there was the actual peak itself, of no very great height, but without any cover to conceal me. Those were the three stages of my journey.

It seemed to me that once I had reached the shelter of the wood all would be easy, for I could lie concealed within its shadows and climb upwards under the cover of night. From eight till twelve would give me four hours of darkness in which to make the ascent. It was only the first stage, then, which I had seriously to consider.

Over that flat country there lay the inviting white road, and I remembered that my comrades had both taken their horses. That was clearly their ruin, for nothing could be easier than for the brigands to keep watch upon the road, and to lay an ambush for all who passed along it. It would not be difficult for me to ride across country, and I was well horsed at that time, for I had not only Volette and Rataplan, who were two of the finest mounts in the army, but I had the splendid black English hunter which I had taken from Sir Cotton. However, after much thought, I determined to go upon foot, since I should then be in a better state to take advantage of any chance which might offer. As to my dress, I covered my Hussar uniform with a long cloak, and I put a gray forage cap upon my head. You may ask me why I did not dress as a peasant, but I answer that a man of honor has no desire to die the death of a spy. It is one thing to be murdered, and it is another to be justly executed by the laws of war. I would not run the risk of such an end.

In the late afternoon I stole out of the camp and passed through the line of our pickets. Beneath my cloak I had a field glass and a pocket pistol, as well as my sword. In my pocket were tinder, flint, and steel.

For two or three miles I kept under cover of the vineyards, and made such good progress that my heart was high within me, and I thought to myself that it only needed a man of some brains to take the matter in hand to bring it easily to success. Of course, Cortex and Duplessis galloping down the high road would be easily seen, but the intelligent

Gerard lurking among the vines was quite another person. I dare say I had got as far as five miles before I met any check. At that point there is a small wine house, round which I perceived some carts and a number of people, the first that I had seen. Now that I was well outside the lines I knew that every person was my enemy, so I crouched lower while I stole along to a point from which I could get a better view of what was going on. I then perceived that these people were peasants, who were loading two wagons with empty wine casks. I failed to see how they could either help or hinder me, so I continued upon my way.

But soon I understood that my task was not so simple as had appeared. As the ground rose, the vineyards ceased, and I came upon a stretch of open country studded with low hills. Crouching in a ditch I examined them with a glass, and I very soon perceived that there was a watcher upon every one of them, and that these people had a line of pickets and outposts thrown forward exactly like our own. I had heard of the discipline which was practiced by this scoundrel whom they called "The Smiler," and this, no doubt, was an example of it. Between the hills there was a cordon of sentries, and, though I worked some distance round to the flank, I still found myself faced by the enemy. It was a puzzle what to do. There was so little cover that a rat could hardly cross without being seen. Of course, it would be easy enough to slip through at night, as I had done with the English at Torres Vedras; but I was still far from the mountain, and I could not in that case reach it in time to light the midnight beacon. I lay in my ditch and I made a thousand plans, each more dangerous than the last. And then suddenly I had that flash of light which comes to the brave man who refuses to despair.

You remember I have mentioned that two wagons were loading up with empty casks at the inn. The heads of the oxen were turned to the east, and it was evident that those wagons were going in the direction which I desired. Could I only conceal myself upon one of them, what better and easier way could I find of passing through the lines of the guerillas? So simple and so good was the plan that I could not restrain a cry of delight as it crossed my mind, and I hurried away instantly in the direction of the inn. There, from behind some bushes, I had a good look at what was going on upon the road.

There were three peasants with red montero caps loading the barrels, and they had completed one wagon and the lower tier of the other. A number of empty barrels still lay outside the wine house waiting to be put on. Fortune was my friend—I have always said that she is a woman and cannot resist a dashing young Hussar. As I watched, the three fellows went into the inn, for the day was hot, and they were thirsty after their labor. Quick as a flash I darted out from my hiding place, climbed on to the wagon, and crept into one of the empty casks. It had a bottom but no top, and it lay upon its side with the open end inwards. There I crouched like a dog in its kennel, my knees drawn up to my chin; for the barrels were not very large and I am a well-grown man. As I lay there, out came the three peasants again, and presently I heard a crash upon the top of me, which told that I had another barrel above me. They piled them upon the cart until I could not imagine how I was ever to get out again. However, it is time to think of crossing the Vistula when you are over the Rhine, and I had no doubt that if chance and my own wits had carried me so far they would carry me farther.

Soon, when the wagon was full, they set forth upon their way, and I within my barrel chuckled at every step, for it was carrying me whither I wished to go. We traveled slowly, and the peasants walked beside the wagons. This I knew, because I heard their voices close to me. They seemed to me to be very merry fellows, for they laughed heartily as they went. What the joke was I could not understand. Though I speak their language fairly well, I could not hear anything comic in the scraps of their conversation which met my ear.

I reckoned that at the rate of walking of a team of oxen we covered about two miles an hour. Therefore, when I was sure that two and a half hours had passed—such hours, my friends, cramped, suffocated, and nearly poisoned with the fumes of the lees—when they had passed, I was sure that the dangerous open country was behind us, and that we were upon the edge of the forest and the mountain. So now I had to turn my mind upon how I was to get out of my barrel. I had thought of several ways, and was balancing one against the other, when the question was decided for me in a very simple but unexpected manner.

The wagon stopped suddenly with a jerk, and I heard a number of gruff voices in excited talk. "Where, where?" cried one. "On our cart," said another. "Who is he?" said a third. "A French officer; I saw his cap and his boots." They all roared with laughter. "I was looking out of the window of the *posada* and I saw him spring into the cask like a toreador with a Seville bull at his heels." "Which cask, then?" "It was this one," said the fellow, and, sure enough, his fist struck the wood beside my head.

What a situation, my friends, for a man of my standing! I blush now, after forty years, when I think of it. To be trussed like a fowl and to listen helplessly to the rude laughter of these boors—to know, too, that my mission had come to an ignominious and even ridiculous end. I would have blessed the man who would have sent a bullet through the cask and freed me from my misery.

I heard the crashing of the barrels as they hurled them off the wagon, and then a couple of bearded faces and the muzzles of two guns looked in at me. They seized me by the sleeves of my coat, and they dragged me out into the daylight. A strange figure I must have looked as I stood blinking and gaping in the blinding sunlight. My body was bent like a cripple's, for I could not straighten my stiff joints, and half my coat was as red as an English soldier's from the lees in which I had lain. They laughed and laughed, these dogs, and as I tried to express by my bearing and gestures the contempt in which I held them, their laughter grew all the louder. But even in these hard circumstances I bore myself like the man I am, and as I cast my eye slowly round I did not find that any of the laughers were very ready to face it.

That one glance round was enough to tell me exactly how I was situated. I had been betrayed by these peasants into the hands of an outpost of guerillas. There were eight of them, savage looking, hairy creatures, with cotton handkerchiefs under their sombreros, and many-buttoned jackets with colored sashes round the waist. Each had a gun and one or two pistols stuck in his girdle. The leader, a great bearded ruffian, held his gun against my ear while the others searched my pockets, taking from me my overcoat, my pistol, my glass, my sword, and, worst of all, my flint and steel and tinder. Come what might I was ruined, for I had no longer the means of lighting the beacon even if I should reach it.

Eight of them, my friends, with three peasants, and I unarmed! Was Etienne Gerard in despair? Did he lose his wits? Ah, you know me too well; but they did not know me yet, these dogs of brigands. Never have I made so supreme and astounding an effort as at this very instant when all seemed lost. Yet you might guess many times before you would hit upon the device by which I escaped them. Listen and I will tell you.

They had dragged me from the wagon when they searched me, and I stood, still twisted and warped, in the midst of them. But the stiffness was wearing off, and already my mind was very actively looking out for some method of breaking away. It was a narrow pass in which the brigands had their outpost. It was bounded on the one hand by a steep mountain side. On the other the ground fell away in a very long slope, which ended in a bushy valley many hundreds of feet below. These fellows, you understand, were hardy mountaineers, who could travel either uphill or down very much quicker than I. They wore abarcas, or shoes of skin, tied on like sandals, which gave them a foothold everywhere. A less resolute man would have despaired. But in an instant I saw and used the strange chance which Fortune had placed in my way. On the very edge of the slope was one of the wine barrels. I moved slowly towards it, and then with a tiger spring I dived into it feet foremost, and with a roll of my body I tipped it over the side of the hill.

Shall I ever forget that dreadful journey—how I bounded and crashed and whizzed down that terrible slope? I had dug in my knees and elbows, bunching my body into a compact bundle so as to steady it; but my head projected from the end, and it was a marvel that I did not dash out my brains. There were long, smooth slopes and then came steeper scarps where the barrel ceased to roll, and sprang into the air like a goat, coming down with a rattle and crash which jarred every bone in my body. How the wind whistled in my ears, and my head turned and turned until I was sick and giddy and nearly senseless! Then, with a swish and a great rasping and crackling of branches, I reached the bushes which I had seen so far below me. Through them I broke my way, down a slope beyond, and deep into another patch of underwood, where striking a sapling my barrel flew to pieces. From amid a heap of staves and hoops I crawled out, my body aching in every inch of it, but my heart singing loudly with joy and my spirit high within me, for I knew how great was the feat which I had accomplished, and I already seemed to see the beacon blazing on the hill.

A horrible nausea had seized me from the tossing which I had undergone, and I felt as I did upon the ocean when first I experienced those movements of which the English have taken so perfidious an advantage. I had to sit for a few moments with my head upon my hands beside the ruins of my barrel. But there was no time for rest. Already I heard shouts above me which told that my pursuers were descending the hill. I dashed into the thickest part of the underwood, and I ran and ran until I was utterly exhausted. Then I lay panting and listened with all my ears, but no sound came to them. I had shaken off my enemies.

When I had recovered my breath I traveled swiftly on, and waded knee-deep through several brooks, for it came into my head that they might follow me with dogs. On gaining a clear place and looking round me, I found to my delight that in spite of my adventures I had not been much out of my way. Above me towered the peak of Merodal, with its bare and bold summit shooting out of the groves of dwarf oaks which shrouded its flanks. These groves were the continuation of the cover under which I found myself, and it seemed to me that I had nothing to fear now until I reached the other side of the forest. At the same time I knew that every man's hand was against me, that I was unarmed, and that there were many people about me. I saw no one, but several times I heard shrill whistles, and once the sound of a gun in the distance.

It was hard work pushing one's way through the bushes, and so I was glad when I came to the larger trees and found a path which led between them. Of course, I was too wise to walk upon it, but I kept near it and followed its course. I had gone some distance, and had, as I imagined, nearly reached the limit of the wood, when a strange, moaning sound fell upon my ears. At first I thought it was the cry of some animals, but then there came words, of which I only caught the French exclamation, "Mon Dieu!" With great caution I advanced in the direction from which the sound proceeded, and this is what I saw.

On a couch of dried leaves there was stretched a man dressed in the same gray uniform which I wore myself. He was evidently horribly wounded, for he held a cloth to his breast which was crimson with his blood. A pool had formed all round his couch, and he lay in a haze of flies, whose buzzing and droning would certainly have called my attention if his groans had not come to my ear. I lay for a moment, fearing some trap, and then, my pity and loyalty rising above all other feelings, I ran forward and knelt by his side. He turned a haggard face upon me, and it was Duplessis, the man who had gone before me. It needed but one glance at his sunken cheeks and glazing eyes to tell me that he was dying.

"Gerard!" said he; "Gerard!"

I could but look my sympathy, but he, though the life was ebbing swiftly out of him, still kept his duty before him, like the gallant gentleman he was.

"The beacon, Gerard! You will light it?"

"Have you flint and steel?"

"It is here."

"Then I will light it tonight."

"I die happy to hear you say so. They shot me, Gerard. But you will tell the Marshal that I did my best."

"And Cortex?"

"He was less fortunate. He fell into their hands and died horribly. If you see that you cannot get away, Gerard, put a bullet into your own heart. Don't die as Cortex did."

I could see that his breath was failing, and I bent low to catch his words.

"Can you tell me anything which can help me in my task?" I asked.

"Yes, yes; De Pombal. He will help you. Trust De Pombal." With the words his head fell back and he was dead.

"Trust De Pombal. It is good advice." To my amazement a man was standing at the very side of me. So absorbed had I been in my comrade's words and intent on his advice that he had crept up without my observing him. Now I sprang to my feet and faced him. He was a tall, dark fellow, black-haired, black-eyed, black-bearded, with a long, sad face. In his hand he had a wine bottle and over his shoulder was slung one of the trebucos, or blunderbusses, which these fellows bear. He made no effort to unsling it, and I understood that this was the man to whom my dead friend had commended me.

"Alas, he is gone!" said he, bending over Duplessis. "He fled into the wood after he was shot, but I was fortunate enough to find where he had fallen and to make his last hours more easy. This couch was my making, and I had brought this wine to slake his thirst.''

"Sir," said I, "in the name of France I thank you. I am but a colonel of light cavalry, but I am Etienne Gerard, and the name stands for something in the French army. May I ask—"

"Yes, sir, I am Aloysius de Pombal, younger brother of the famous nobleman of that name. At present I am the first lieutenant in the band of the guerilla chief who is usually known as Manuelo, 'The Smiler.' "

My word, I clapped my hand to the place where my pistol should have been, but the man only smiled at the gesture.

"I am his first lieutenant, but I am also his deadly enemy," said he. He slipped off his jacket and pulled up his shirt as he spoke. "Look at this!" he cried, and he turned upon me a back which was all scored and lacerated with red and purple weals. "This is what 'The Smiler' has done to me, a man with the noblest blood of Portugal in my veins. What I will do to 'The Smiler' you have still to see."

There was such fury in his eyes and in the grin of his white teeth that I could no longer doubt his truth, with that clotted and oozing back to corroborate his words.

"I have ten men sworn to stand by me," said he. "In a few days I hope to join your army, when I have done my work here. In the meanwhile—" A strange change came over his face, and he suddenly slung his musket to the front: "Hold up your hands, you French hound!" he yelled. "Up with them, or I blow your head off!"

98

You start, my friends! You stare! Think, then, how I stared and started at this sudden ending of our talk. There was the black muzzle, and there the dark, angry eyes behind it. What could I do? I was helpless. I raised my hands in the air. At the same moment voices sounded from all parts of the wood, there were crying and calling and rushing of many feet. A swarm of dreadful figures broke through the green bushes, a dozen hands seized me, and I, poor, luckless, frenzied I, was a prisoner once more. Thank God there was no pistol which I could have plucked from my belt and snapped at my own head. Had I been armed at that moment I should not be sitting here in this café and telling you these old-world tales.

With grimy, hairy hands clutching me on every side I was led along the pathway through the wood, the villain De Pombal giving directions to my captors. Four of the brigands carried up the dead body of Duplessis. The shadows of evening were already falling when we cleared the forest and came out upon the mountain side. Up this I was driven until we reached the headquarters of the guerillas, which lay in a cleft close to the summit of the mountain. There was the beacon which had cost me so much, a square stack of wood, immediately above our heads. Below were two or three huts which had belonged, no doubt, to goatherds, and which were now used to shelter these rascals. Into one of these I was cast, bound and helpless, and the dead body of my poor comrade was laid beside me.

I was lying there with the one thought still consuming me, how to wait a few hours and to get at that pile of faggots above my head, when the door of my prison opened and a man entered. Had my hands been free I should have flown at his throat, for it was none other than De Pombal. A couple of brigands were at his heels, but he ordered them back and closed the door behind him.

"You villain!" said I.

"Hush!" he cried. "Speak low, for I do not know who may be listening, and my life is at stake. I have some words to say to you, Colonel Gerard; I wish well to you, as I did to your dead companion. As I spoke to you beside his body I saw that we were surrounded, and that your capture was unavoidable. I should have shared your fate had I hesitated. I instantly captured you myself, so as to preserve the confidence of the band. Your own sense will tell you that there was nothing else for me to do. I do not know now whether I can save you, but at least I will try."

This was a new light upon the situation. I told him that I could not tell how far he spoke the truth, but that I would judge him by his actions.

"I ask nothing better," said he. "A word of advice to you! The chief will see you now. Speak him fair, or he will have you sawn between two planks. Contradict nothing he says. Give him such information he wants. It is your only chance. If you can gain time something may come in our favor. Now, I have no more time. Come at once, or suspicion may be awakened." He helped me to rise and then, opening the door, he dragged me out very roughly, and with the aid of the fellows outside he brutally pushed and thrust me to the place where the guerilla chief was seated, with his rude followers gathered round him.

A remarkable man was Manuelo, "The Smiler." He was fat and florid and comfortable, with a big, clean-shaven face and a bald head, the very model of a kindly father of a family. As I looked at his honest smile I could scarcely believe that this was, indeed, the infamous ruffian whose name was a horror through the English Army as well as our own. It is well known that Trent, who was a British officer, afterwards had the fellow hanged for his brutalities. He sat upon a boulder and he beamed upon me like one who meets an old acquaintance. I observed, however, that one of his men leaned upon a long saw, and the sight was enough to cure me of all delusions.

"Good evening, Colonel Gerard," said he. "We have been highly honored by General Massena's staff: Major Cortex one day, Colonel Duplessis the next, and now Colonel Gerard. Possibly the Marshal himself may be induced to honor us with a visit. You have seen Duplessis, I understand. Cortex you will find nailed to a tree down yonder. It only remains to be decided how we can best dispose of yourself."

It was not a cheering speech; but all the time his fat face was wretched in smiles, and he lisped out his words in the most mincing and amiable fashion. Now, however, he suddenly leaned forward, and I read a very real intensity in his eyes.

"Colonel Gerard," said he, "I cannot promise you your life, for it is not our custom, but I can give you an easy death or I can give you a terrible one. Which shall it be?"

"What do you wish me to do in exchange?"

"If you would die easy I ask you to give me truthful answers to the questions which I ask."

A sudden thought flashed through my mind.

"You wish to kill me," said I; "it cannot matter to you how I die. If I answer your questions, will you let me choose the manner of my own death?"

"Yes, I will," said he, "so long as it is before midnight tonight."

"Swear it!" I cried.

"The word of a Portuguese gentleman is sufficient," said he.

"Not a word will I say until you have sworn it."

He flushed with anger and his eyes swept round towards the saw. But he understood from my tone that I meant what I said, and that I was not a man to be bullied into submission. He pulled a cross from under his zammara or jacket of black sheepskin.

"I swear it," said he.

Oh, my joy as I heard the words! What an end —what an end for the first swordsman of France! I could have laughed with delight at the thought.

"Now, your questions!" said I.

"You swear in turn to answer them truly?"

"I do, upon the honor of a gentleman and a soldier." It was, as you perceive, a terrible thing that I promised, but what was it compared to what I might gain by compliance?

"This is a very fair and a very interesting bargain," said he, taking a notebook from his pocket. "Would you kindly turn your gaze towards the French camp?"

Following the direction of his gesture, I turned and looked down upon the camp in the plain beneath us. In spite of the fifteen miles, one could in that clear atmosphere see every detail with the utmost distinctness. There were the long squares of our tents and our huts, with the cavalry lines and the dark patches which marked the ten batteries of artillery. How sad to think of my magnificent regiment waiting down yonder, and to know that they would never see their colonel again! With one squadron of them I could have swept all these cutthroats off the face of the earth. My eager eyes filled with tears as I looked at the corner of the camp where I knew that there were eight hundred men, any one of whom would have died for his colonel. But my sadness vanished when I saw behind the tents the plumes of smoke which marked the headquarters at Torres Novas. There was Massena, and, please God, at the cost of my life his mission would that night be done. A spasm of pride and exultation filled my breast. I should have liked to have had a voice of thunder that I might call to them, "Behold it is I, Etienne Gerard, who will die in order to save the army of Clausel!" It was, indeed, sad to think that so noble a deed should be done, and that no one should be there to tell the tale.

"Now," said the brigand chief, "you see the camp and you see also the road which leads to Coimbra. It is crowded with your fourgons and your ambulances. Does this mean that Massena is about to retreat?"

One could see the dark moving lines of wagons with an occasional flash of steel from the escort. There could, apart from my promise, be no indiscretion in admitting that which was already obvious.

"He will retreat," said I.

"By Coimbra?"

"I believe so."

"But the army of Clausel?"

I shrugged my shoulders.

"Every path to the south is blocked. No message can reach them. If Massena falls back the army of Clausel is doomed."

"It must take its chance," said I.

"How many men has he?"

"I should say about fourteen thousand."

"How much cavalry?"

"One brigade of Montbrun's Division."

"What regiments?"

"The 4th Chasseurs, the 9th Hussars, and a regiment of Cuirassiers."

"Quite right," said he, looking at his notebook "I can tell you speak the truth, and heaven help you if you don't." Then, division by division, he went over the whole army, asking the composition of each brigade. Need I tell you that I would have had my tongue torn out before I would have told him such things had I not a greater end in view? I would let him know all if I could but save the army of Clausel.

At last he closed his notebook and replaced it in his pocket. "I am obliged to you for this information, which shall reach Lord Wellington tomorrow," said he. "You have done your share of the bargain; it is for me now to perform mine. How would you wish to die? As a soldier you would, no doubt, prefer to be shot, but some think that a jump over the Merodal precipice is really an easier death. A good few have taken it, but w·

were, unfortunately, never able to get an opinion from them afterwards. There is the saw, too, which does not appear to be popular. We could hang you, no doubt, but it would involve the inconvenience of going down to the wood. However, a promise is a promise, and you seem to be an excellent fellow, so we will spare no pains to meet your wishes."

"You said," I answered, "that I must die before midnight. I will choose, therefore, just one minute before that hour."

"Very good," said he. "Such clinging to life is rather childish, but your wishes shall be met."

"As to the method," I added, "I love a death which all the world can see. Put me on yonder pile of faggots and burn me alive, as saints and martyrs have been burned before me. That is no common end, but one which an Emperor might envy."

The idea seemed to amuse him very much.

"Why not?" said he. "If Massena has sent you to spy upon us, he may guess what the fire upon the mountains means."

"Exactly," said I. "You have hit upon my very reason. He will guess, and all will know, that I have died a soldier's death."

"I see no objection whatever," said the brigand, with his abominable smile. "I will send some goat's flesh and wine into your hut. The sun is sinking, and it is nearly eight o'clock. In four hours be ready for your end."

It was a beautiful world to be leaving. I looked at the golden haze below, where the last rays of the sinking sun shone upon the blue waters of the winding Tagus and gleamed upon the white sails of the English transports. Very beautiful it was, and very sad to leave; but there are things more beautiful than that. The death that is died for the sake of others, honor, and duty, and loyalty, and love—these are the beauties far brighter than any which the eye can see. My breast was filled with admiration for my own most noble conduct, and with wonder whether any soul would ever come to know how I had placed myself in the heart of the beacon which saved the army of Clausel. I hoped so and I prayed so, for what a consolation it would be to my mother, what an example to the army, what a pride to my Hussars! When De Pombal came at last into my hut with the food and the wine, the first request I made him was that he would write an account of my death and send it to the French camp. He answered not a word, but I ate my supper with a better appetite from the thought that my glorious fate would not be altogether unknown.

I had been there about two hours when the door opened again, and the chief stood looking in. I was in darkness, but a brigand with a torch stood beside him, and I saw his eyes and his teeth gleaming as he peered at me.

"Ready?" he asked.

"It is not yet time."

"You stand out for the last minute?"

"A promise is a promise."

"Very good. Be it so. We have a little justice to do among ourselves, for one of my fellows has been misbehaving. We have a strict rule of our own which is no respecter of persons, as De Pombal here could tell you. Do you truss him and lay him on the faggots, De Pombal, and I will return to see him die.''

De Pombal and the man with the torch entered, while I heard the steps of the chief passing away. De Pombal closed the door.

''Colonel Gerard,'' said he, ''you must trust this man, for he is one of my party. It is neck or nothing. We may save you yet. But I take a great risk, and I want a definite promise. If we save you, will you guarantee that we have a friendly reception in the French camp and that all the past will be forgotten?''

''I do guarantee it.''

''And I trust your honor. Now, quick, quick, there is not an instant to lose! If this monster returns we shall die horribly, all three.''

I stared in amazement at what he did. Catching up a long rope he wound it round the body of my dead comrade, and he tied a cloth round his mouth so to almost cover his face.

''Do you lie there!'' he cried, and he laid me in the place of the dead body. ''I have four of my men waiting, and they will place this upon the beacon.'' He opened the door and gave an order. Several of the brigands entered and bore out Duplessis. For myself I remained upon the floor, with my mind in a turmoil of hope and wonder.

Five minutes later De Pombal and his men were back.

''You are laid upon the beacon,'' said he; ''I defy anyone in the world to say it is not you, and you are so gagged and bound that no one can expect you to speak or move. Now, it only remains to carry forth the body of Duplessis and to toss it over the Merodal precipice.''

Two of them seized me by the head and two by the heels and carried me, stiff and inert, from the hut. As I came into the open air I could have cried out in my amazement. The moon had risen, above the beacon, and there, clearly outlined against its silver light, was the figure of the man stretched upon the top. The brigands were either in their camp or standing round the beacon, for none of them stopped or questioned our little party. De Pombal led them in the direction of the precipice. At the brow we were out of sight, and there I was allowed to use my feet once more. De Pombal pointed to a narrow, winding track.

''This is the way down,'' said he, and then suddenly, ''Dios mio, what is that?''

A terrible cry had risen out of the woods beneath us. I saw that De Pombal was shivering like a frightened horse.

''It is that devil,'' he whispered. ''He ·' treating another as he treated me. But on, on for Heaven help us if he lays his hands upon us!''

One by one we crawled down the narrow goat track. At the bottom of the cliff we were back in the woods once more. Suddenly a yellow glare shone above us, and the black shadows of the tree-trunks started out in front. They had fired the beacon behind us. Even from where we stood we could see that impassive body amid the flames, and the black figures of the guerillas as they danced, howling like cannibals, round the pile. Ha! How I shook my fist at them, the dogs, and how I vowed that one day my Hussars and I would make the reckoning level!

De Pombal knew how the outposts were placed and all the paths which led through the forest. But to avoid these villains we had to plunge among the hills and walk for many a weary mile. And yet how gladly would I have walked those extra leagues if only for one sight which they brought to my eyes! It may have been two o'clock in the morning when we halted upon the bare shoulder of a hill over which our path curled. Looking back we saw the red glow of the embers of the beacon as if volcanic fires were bursting from the tall peak of Merodal. And then, as I gazed, I saw something else—something which caused me to shriek with joy and to fall upon the ground, rolling in my delight. For, far away upon the southern horizon, there winked and twinkled one great yellow light throbbing and flaming, the light of no house, the light of no star, but the answering beacon of Mount d'Ossa, which told that the army of Clausel knew what Etienne Gerard had been sent to tell them.

Stanley Weyman
The King's Stratagem

In the days when Henry the Fourth of France was as yet King of Navarre only, and in that little kingdom of hills and woods which occupies the southwestern corner of the larger country, was with difficulty supporting the Huguenot cause against the French court and the Catholic League—in the days when every little moated town, from the Dordogne to the Pyrenees, was a bone of contention between the young king and the crafty queen mother, Catherine de Medicis, a conference between these warring personages took place in the picturesque town of La Réole And great was the fame of it.

La Réole still rises gray, timeworn, and half-ruined on a lofty cliff above the broad green waters of the Garonne, forty-odd miles from Bordeaux. It is a small place now, but in the days of which we are speaking it was important, strongly fortified, and guarded by a castle which looked down on some hundreds of red-tiled roofs, rising in terraces from the river. As the meeting place of the two sovereigns it was for the time as gay as Paris itself. Catherine had brought with her a bevy of fair maids of honor, and trusted more perhaps in the effect of their charms than in her own diplomacy. But the peaceful appearance of the town was as delusive as the smooth bosom of the Gironde; for even while every other house in its streets rang with music and silvery laughter, each party was ready to fly to arms at a word if it saw that any advantage could be gained thereby.

On an evening shortly before the end of the conference, two men were seated at play in a room, the deep-embrasured window of which looked down from a considerable height upon the river. The hour was late; below them the town lay silent. Outside, the moonlight fell bright and pure on sleeping fields, on vineyards, and dark far-spreading woods. Within the room a silver lamp suspended from the ceiling threw light upon the table, but left the farther parts of the chamber in shadow. The walls were hung with faded tapestry, and on a low bedstead in one corner lay a handsome cloak, a sword, and one of the clumsy pistols of the period. Across a high-backed chair lay another cloak and sword, and on the window seat, beside a pair of saddlebags, were strewn half a dozen trifles such as soldiers carried from cap to camp—a silver comfit box, a jeweled dagger, a mask, a velvet cap.

The faces of the players, as they bent over the cards, were in shadow. One—a slight, dark man of middle height, with a weak chin—and a mouth that would have equally betrayed its weakness had it not been shaded by a dark mustache—seemed, from the occasional oaths which he let drop, to be losing heavily. Yet his opponent, a stouter and darker man, with a sword cut across his left temple, and the swaggering air that has at all times marked the professional soldier, showed no signs of triumph or elation. On the contrary, though he kept silence, or spoke only a formal word or two, there was a gleam of anxiety and suppressed excitement in his eyes; and more than once he looked keenly at his companion, as if to judge of his feelings or to learn whether the time had come for some experiment which he meditated. But for this, an observer looking in through the window would have taken the two for that common conjunction—the hawk and the pigeon.

At last the younger player threw down his cards, with an exclamation.

"You have the luck of the evil one," he said, bitterly. "How much is that?"

"Two thousand crowns," the other replied without emotion. "You will play no more?"

"No! I wish to Heaven I had never played at all!" was the answer. As he spoke the loser rose, and moving to the window stood looking out. For a few moments the elder man remained in his seat, gazing furtively at him; at length he too rose, and, stepping softly to his companion, he touched him on the shoulder. "Your pardon a moment, M. le Vicomte," he said. "Am I right in concluding that the loss of this sum will inconvenience you?"

"A thousand fiends!" the young gamester exclaimed, turning on him wrathfully. "Is there any man whom the loss of two thousand crowns would not inconvenience? As for me—"

"For you," the other continued smoothly, filling up the pause, "shall I be wrong in supposing that it means something like ruin?"

"Well, sir, and if it does?" the young man retorted, and he drew himself up, his cheek a shade paler with passion. "Depend upon it you shall be paid. Do not be afraid of that!"

"Gently, gently, my friend," the winner answered, his patience in strong contrast to the other's violence. "I had no intention of insulting you, believe me. Those who play with the Vicomte de Noirterre are not wont to doubt his honor. I spoke only in your own interest. It has occurred to me, Vicomte, that the matter may be arranged at less cost to yourself."

"How?" was the curt question.

"May I speak freely?" The Vicomte shrugged his shoulders, and the other, taking silence for consent, proceeded: "You, Vicomte, are governor of Lusigny for the King of Navarre; I, of Créance, for the King of France. Our towns lie but three leagues apart. Could I by any chance, say on one of these fine nights, make myself master of Lusigny, it would be worth more than two thousand crowns to me. Do you understand?"

"No," the young man answered slowly, "I do not."

"Think over what I have said, then," was the brief answer.

For a full minute there was silence in the room.

The Vicomte gazed from the window with knitted brows and compressed lips, while his companion, seated near at hand, leaned back in his chair, with an air of affected carefulness. Outside, the rattle of arms and hum of voices told that the watch were passing through the street. The church bell rang one o'clock. Suddenly the Vicomte burst into a forced laugh, and, turning, took up his cloak and sword. "The trap was well laid, M. le Capitaine," he said almost jovially; "but I am still sober enough to take care of myself—and of Lusigny. I wish you good night. You shall have your money, do not fear."

"Still, I am afraid it will cost you dearly," the Captain answered, as he rose and moved towards the door to open it for his guest. And then, when his hand was already on the latch, he paused. "My lord," he said, "what do you say to this, then? I will stake the two thousand crowns you have lost to me, and another thousand to boot— against your town. Oh, no one can hear us. If you win you go off a free man with my thousand. If you lose, you put me in possession—one of these fine nights. Now, that is an offer. What do you say to it? A single hand to decide."

The younger man's face reddened. He turned; his eyes sought the table and the cards; he stood irresolute. The temptation came at an unfortunate moment; a moment when the excitement of play had given way to depression, and he saw nothing outside the door, on the latch of which his hand was laid, but the bleak reality of ruin. The temptation to return, the thought that by a single hand he might set himself right with the world was too much for him. Slowly—he came back to the table. "Confound you!" he said passionately. "I think you are the devil himself!"

"Don't talk child's talk!" the other answered coldly, drawing back as his victim advanced. "If you do not like the offer you need not take it."

But the young man was a born gambler, and his fingers had already closed on the cards. Picking them up idly he dropped them once, twice, thrice on the table, his eyes gleaming with the play fever. "If I win?" he said doubtfully. "What then? Let us have it quite clearly."

"You carry away a thousand crowns," the Captain answered quietly. "If you lose, you contrive to leave one of the gates of Lusigny open for me before next full moon. That is all."

"And what if I lose, and do not pay the forfeit?" the Vicomte asked, laughing weakly.

"I trust to your honor," the Captain answered. And, strange as it may seem, he knew his man. The young noble of the day might betray his cause and his trust, but the debt of honor incurred at play was binding on him.

"Well," said the Vicomte, with a deep breath, "I agree. Who is to deal?"

"As you will," the Captain replied, masking under an appearance of indifference an excitement which darkened his cheek, and caused the pulse in the old wound on his face to beat furiously.

"Then do you deal," said the Vicomte.

"With your permission," the Captain assented. And gathering the cards he dealt with them a practiced hand, and pushed his opponent's six across to him.

The young man took up the hand and, as he sorted it, and looked from it to his companion's face, he repressed a groan with difficulty. The moonlight shining through the casement fell in silvery sheen on a few feet of the floor. With the light something of the silence and coolness of the night entered also, and appealed to him. For a few seconds he hesitated. He made even as if he would have replaced the hand on the table. But he had gone too far to retrace his steps with honor. It was too late, and with a muttered word, which his dry lips refused to articulate, he played the first card.

He took that trick and the next; they were secure.

"And now?" said the Captain who knew well where the pinch came. "What next?"

The Vicomte compressed his lips. Two courses were open to him. By adopting one he could almost for certain win one more trick. By the other he might just possibly win two tricks. He was a gamester, he adopted the latter course. In half a minute it was over. He had lost.

The winner nodded gravely. "The luck is with me still," he said, keeping his eyes on the table that the light of triumph which had leaped into them might not be seen. "When do you go back to your command, Vicomte?"

The unhappy man sat, as one stunned, his eyes on the painted cards which had cost him so dearly. "The day after tomorrow," he muttered at last, striving to collect himself.

"Then shall we say—the following evening?" the Captain asked, courteously.

The young man shivered. "As you will," he muttered.

"We quite understand one another," continued the winner, eyeing his man watchfully, and speaking with more urgency. "I may depend on you, M. le Vicomte, I presume—to keep your word?"

"The Noirterres have never been wanting to their word," the young nobleman answered, stung into passing passion. "If I live, I will put Lusigny into your hands, M. le Capitaine. Afterwards I will do my best to recover it—in another way."

"I shall be most happy to meet you in that way," replied the Captain, bowing lightly. And in one more minute, the door of his lodging had closed on the other; and he was alone—alone with his triumph, his ambition, his hopes for the future— alone with the greatness to which his capture of Lusigny was to be the first step. He would enjoy the greatness not a whit the less because fortune had hitherto dealt out to him more blows than caresses, and he was still at forty, after a score of years of roughest service, the governor of a paltry country town.

Meanwhile, in the darkness of the narrow streets, the Vicomte was making his way to his lodgings in a state of despair difficult to describe, impossible to exaggerate. Chilled, sobered, and affrighted, he looked back and saw how he had thrown for all and lost all, how he had saved the dregs of his fortune at the expense of his loyalty, how he had seen a way of escape—and lost it forever! No wonder that as he trudged through the mud and darkness of the sleeping town his breath came quickly and his chest heaved, and he looked from side to side as a hunted animal might look, uttering great sighs. Ah, if he could have retraced the last three hours! If he could have undone that he had done!

In a fever, he entered his lodging, and securing the door behind him stumbled up the stone stairs and entered his room. The impulse to confide his misfortunes to someone was so strong upon him that he was glad to see a dark form half sitting, half lying in a chair before the dying embers of a wood fire. In those days a man's natural confidant was his valet, the follower, half friend, half servant, who had been born on his estate, who lay on a pallet at the foot of his bed, who carried his *billets-doux* and held his cloak at the duello, who rode near his stirrup in fight and nursed him in illness, who not seldom advised him in the choice of a wife, and lied in support of his suit.

The young Vicomte flung his cloak over a chair. "Get up, you rascal!" he cried impatiently. "You pig, you dog!" he continued, with increasing anger. "Sleeping there as though your master were not ruined by that scoundrel of a Breton! Bah!" he added, gazing bitterly at his follower. "You are of the *canaille,* and have neither honor to lose nor a town to betray!"

The sleeping man moved in his chair but did not awake. The Vicomte, his patience exhausted, snatched the bonnet from his head and threw it on the ground. "Will you listen?" he said. "Or go, if you choose look for another master. I am ruined! Do you hear? Ruined, Gil! I have lost all—money, land, Lusigny itself—at the cards!"

The man, roused at last, stooped with a sleepy

movement, and picking up his hat dusted it with his hand, then rose with a yawn to his feet.

"I am afraid, Vicomte," he said, in tones that, quiet as they were, sounded like thunder in the young man's astonished and bewildered ears, "I am afraid that if you have lost Lusigny—you have lost something which was not yours to lose!"

As he spoke he struck the embers with his boot, and the fire, blazing up, shone on his face. The Vicomte saw, with stupor, that the man before him was not Gil at all—was indeed the last person in the world to whom he should have betrayed himself. The astute smiling eyes, the aquiline nose, the high forehead, and projecting chin, which the short beard and mustache scarcely concealed, were only too well known to him. He stepped back with a cry of despair. "Sir!" he said, and then his tongue failed him. His arms dropped by his sides. He stood silent, pale, convicted, his chin on his breast. The man to whom he had confessed his treachery was the master whom he had agreed to betray.

"I had suspected something of this," Henry of Navarre continued, after a lengthy pause, and with a tinge of irony in his tone. "Rosny told me that that old fox, the Captain of Créance, was affecting your company somewhat too much, M. le Vicomte, and I find that, as usual, his suspicions were well-founded. What with a gentleman who shall be nameless, who has bartered a ford and a castle for the favor of Mademoiselle de Luynes, and yourself, and another I know of—I am blessed with some faithful followers, it seems! For shame! For shame, sir!" he continued, seating himself with dignity in the chair from which he had risen, but turning it so that he confronted his host. "Have you nothing to say for yourself?"

The young noble stood with bowed head, his face white. This was ruin, indeed, absolute irremediable ruin. "Sir," he said at last, "your Majesty has a right to my life, not to my honor."

"Your honor!" Henry exclaimed, biting contempt in his tone.

The young man started, and for a second his cheek flamed under the well-deserved reproach; but he recovered himself. "My debt to your Majesty," he said, "I am willing to pay."

"Since pay you must," Henry muttered softly.

"But I claim to pay also my debt to the Captain of Créance."

The King of Navarre stared. "Oh," he said. "So you would have me take your worthless life, and give up Lusigny?"

"I am in your hands, sire."

"Pish, sir!" Henry replied in angry astonishment. "You talk like a child. Such an offer, M. de Noirterre, is folly, and you know it. Now listen to me. It was lucky for you that I came in tonight, intending to question you. Your madness is known to me only, and I am willing to overlook it. Do you hear? I am willing to pardon. Cheer up, therefore, and be a man. You are young; I forgive you. This shall be between you and me only," the young prince continued, his eyes softening as the other's head sank lower, "and you need think no more of it until the day when I shall say to you, 'Now, M. de Noirterre, for Navarre and for Henry, strike!'"

He rose as the last words passed his lips, and held out his hand. The Vicomte fell on one knee, and kissed it reverently, then sprang to his feet again. "Sire," he said, his eyes shining, "you have punished me heavily, more heavily than was needful. There is only one way in which I can show my gratitude, and that is by ridding you of a servant who can never again look your enemies in the face."

"What new folly is this?" Henry asked sternly. "Do you not understand that I have forgiven you?"

"Therefore I cannot give up Lusigny to the enemy, and I must acquit myself of my debt to the Captain of Créance in the only way which remains," the young man replied firmly. "Death is not so hard that I would not meet it twice over rather than again betray my trust."

"This is midsummer madness!" said the King, hotly.

"Possibly," replied the Vicomte, without emotion; "yet of a kind to which your Grace is not altogether a stranger."

The words appealed to that love of the fanciful and the chivalrous which formed part of the young King's nature, and was one cause alike of his weakness and his strength. In its more extravagant flights it gave opportunity after opportunity to his enemies, in its nobler and saner expressions it won victories which all his astuteness and diplomacy could not have compassed. He stood now, looking with half-hidden admiration at the man whom two minutes before he had despised.

"I think you are in jest," he said presently and with some scorn.

"No, sir," the young man answered, gravely. "In my country they have a proverb about us. 'The Noirterres,' say they, 'have ever been bad players but good payers.' I will not be the first to be worse than my name!"

He spoke with so quiet a determination that the King was staggered, and for a minute or two paced the room in silence, inwardly reviling the obstinacy of this weak-kneed supporter, yet unable to withold his admiration from it. At length he stopped, with a low exclamation.

"Wait!" he cried. "I have it! *Ventre Saint Gris,* man, I have it!" His eyes sparkled, and, with a gentle laugh, he hit the table a sounding blow. "Ha! ha! I have it!" he repeated gaily.

The young noble gazed at him in surprise, half suspicious, half incredulous. But when Henry in low, rapid tones had expounded his plan, the young man's face underwent a change. Hope and life sprang into it. The blood flew to his cheeks. His whole aspect softened. In a moment he was on his knee, mumbling the prince's hand, his eyes moist with gratitude. Nor was that all; the two talked long, the murmur of their voices broken more than once by the ripple of laughter. When they at length separated, and Henry, his face hidden by the folds of his cloak, had stolen to his lodgings, where, no doubt, more than one watcher was awaiting him with a mind full of anxious fears, the Vicomte threw open his window and looked out on the night. The moon had set, but the stars still shone peacefully in the dark canopy above. He remembered, his throat choking with silent emotion, that he was looking towards his home—the round towers among the walnut woods of Navarre which had been in his family since the days of St Louis, and which he had so lightly risked. And he registered a vow in his heart that of all Henry's servants he would henceforth be the most faithful.

Meanwhile the Captain of Créance was enjoying the sweets of his coming triumph. He did not look out into the night, it is true—he was over old for sentiment—but pacing up and down the room he planned and calculated, considering how he might make the most of his success. He was still comparatively young. He had years of strength before him. He would rise high and higher. He would not easily be satisfied. The times were troubled, opportunitites were many, fools not few; bold men with brains and hands were rare.

At the same time he knew that he could be sure of nothing until Lusigny was actually in his possession; and he spent the next few days in painful suspense. But no hitch occurred nor seemed likely. The Vicomte made him the necessary communications; and men in his own pay informed him of dispositions ordered by the governor of Lusigny which left him in no doubt that the loser intended to pay his debt.

It was, therefore, with a heart already gay with anticipation that the Captain rode out of Créance two hours before midnight on an evening eight days later. The night was dark, but he knew his road well. He had with him a powerful force, composed in part of thirty of his own garrison, bold hardy fellows, and in part of six score horsemen, lent him by the governor of Montauban. As the Vicomte had undertaken to withdraw, under some pretense or other, one-half of his command and to have one of the gates opened by a trusty hand, the Captain foresaw no difficulty. He trotted along in excellent spirits, now stopping to scan with approval the dark line of his troopers, now to bid them muffle the jingle of their swords and corselets that nevertheless rang sweet music in his ears. He looked for an easy victory; but it was not any slight misadventure that would rob him of his prey. If necessary he would fight and fight hard. Still, as his company wound along the riverside or passed into the black shadow of the oak grove, which stands a mile to the east of Lusigny, he did not expect that there would be much fighting.

Treachery alone, he thought, could thwart him; and of treachery there was no sign. The troopers had scarcely halted under the last clump of trees before a figure detached itself from one of the largest trunks, and advanced to the Captain's rein. The Captain saw with surprise that it was the Vicomte himself. For a second he thought that something had gone wrong but the young noble's first words reassured him. "It is arranged," M. de Noirterre whispered, as the Captain bent down to him. "I have kept my word, and I think that there will be no resistance. The planks for crossing the moat lie opposite the gate. Knock thrice at the latter, and it will be opened. There are not fifty armed men in the place."

"Good!" the Captain answered, in the same cautious tone. "But you—"

"I am believed to be elsewhere, and must be gone. I have far to ride tonight. Farewell."

"Till we meet again," the Captain answered; and without more ado he saw his ally glide away and disappear in the darkness. A cautious word set the troop in motion, and a very few minutes saw them standing on the edge of the moat, the outline of the gateway tower looming above them, a shade darker than the rack of clouds which overhead raced silently across the sky. A moment of suspense while one and another shivered—for there is that in a night attack which touches the nerves of the stoutest—and the planks were found, and as quietly as possible laid across the moat. This was so skillfully done that it evoked no challenge, and the Captain crossing quickly with a few picked men, stood in the twinkling of an eye under the shadow of the gateway. Still no sound was heard, save the hurried breathing of those at his elbow, the stealthy tread of others crossing, the persistent voices of the frogs in the water beneath. Cautiously he knocked three times and waited. The third rap had scarcely sounded before the gate rolled silently open, and he sprang in, followed by his men.

So far so good. A glance at the empty street and the porter's pale face told him at once that the Vicomte had kept his word. But he was too old a soldier to take anything for granted, and forming up his men as quickly as they entered, he allowed no one to advance until all were inside, and then, his trumpet sounding a wild note of defiance, two-thirds of his force sprang forward in a compact body while the other third remained to hold the gate. In a moment the town awoke to find itself in

125

the hands of the enemy.

As the Vicomte had promised, there was no resistance. In the small keep a score of men did indeed run to arms, but only to lay their weapons down without striking a blow when they became aware of the force opposed to them. Their leader sullenly acquiescing, gave up his sword and the keys of the town to the victorious Captain; who, as he sat his horse in the middle of the marketplace, giving his orders and sending off riders with the news, already saw himself in fancy Governor of Angouleme and Knight of the Holy Ghost.

As the red light of the torches fell on steel caps and polished hauberks, on the serried ranks of pike men, and the circle of whitefaced townsfolk, the picturesque old square looked doubly picturesque, and he who sat in the midst, its master, doubly a hero. Every five minutes, with a clatter of iron on the rough pavement and a shower of sparks, a horseman sprang away to tell the news at Montauban or Cahors; and every time that this occurred, the Captain, astride on his charger, felt a new sense of power and triumph.

Suddenly the low murmur of voices about him was broken by a new sound, the distant beat of hoofs, not departing but arriving, and coming each moment nearer. It was but the tramp of a single horse, but there was something in the sound which made the Captain prick his ears, and secured for the arriving messenger a speedy passage through the crowd. Even at the last the man did not spare his horse, but spurred through the ranks to the Captain's very side, and then and then only sprang to the ground. His face was pale, his eyes were bloodshot. His right arm was bound up in bloodstained cloths. With an oath of amazement, the Captain recognized the officer whom he had left in charge of Créance, and he thundered, ''What is this? What is it?''

''They have got Créance!'' the man gasped, reeling as he spoke. ''They have got—Créance!''

''Who?'' the Captain shrieked, his face purple with rage.

''The little man of Béarn! The King of Navarre! He assaulted it five hundred strong an hour after you left, and had the gate down before we could fire a dozen shots. We did what we could, but we were but one to seven. I swear, Captain, that we did all we could. Look at this!''

Almost black in the face, the Captain swore another oath. It was not only that he saw governorship and honors vanish like Will-o'-the-wisps, but that he saw even more quickly that he had made himself the laughingstock of a kingdom! And that was the truth. To this day, among the stories which the southern French love to tell of the prowess and astuteness of their great Henry, there is none more frequently told, none more frequently made the subject of mirth, than that of the famous exchange of Créance for Lusigny; the tradition of the move by which, between dawn and sunrise, without warning, without a word, he gave his opponents mate.

Anthony Hope

The Sin of the
Bishop of Modenstein

In the days of Rudolf III there stood on the hill opposite the Castle of Zenda, and on the other side of the valley in which the town lies, on the site where the chateau of Tarlenheim now is situated, a fine and strong castle belonging to Count Nikolas of Festenburg. He was a noble of very old and high family, and had great estates; his house being, indeed, second only to the Royal House in rank and reputation. He himself was a young man of great accomplishments, of a domineering temper, and of much ambition; and he had gained distinction in the wars that marked the closing years of the reign of King Henry the Lion. With King Rudolf he was not on terms of cordial friendship, for he despised the King's easy manners and carelessness of dignity, while the King had no love for a gentleman whose one object seemed to be to surpass and outshine him in the eyes of his people, and who never rested from extending and fortifying his castle until it threatened to surpass Zenda itself both in strength and magnificence. Moreover Nikolas, although maintaining a state ample and suitable to his rank, was yet careful and prudent, while Rudolf spent all that he received and more besides, so that the Count grew richer and the King poorer. But in spite of these causes of difference, the Count was received at court with apparent graciousness, and no open outburst of enmity had yet occurred, the pair being, on the contrary, often together, and sharing their sports and pastimes with one another.

Now most of these diversions were harmless, or, indeed, becoming and proper, but there was one among them full of danger to a man of hot head and ungoverned impulse such as King Rudolf was. And this one was dicing, in which the King took great delight, and in which Count Nikolas was very ready to encourage him. The King, who was generous and hated to win from poor men or those who might be playing beyond their means in order to give him pleasure, was delighted to find an opponent whose purse was as long or longer than his own, and thus gradually came to pass many evenings with the boxes in Nikolas's company. And the more evenings he passed, the deeper he fell into the Count's debt; for the King drank wine, while the Count was content with small beer, and when the King was losing he doubled his stakes, whereas the Count took in sail if the wind seemed adverse. Thus always and steadily the debt grew, till at last Rudolf dared not reckon how large it had become, nor did he dare to disclose it to his advisers. For there were great public burdens already imposed by reason of King Henry's wars, and the citizens of Strelsau were not in a mood to bear fresh exaction, nor to give their hard earnings for the payment of the King's gambling debts; in fine, although they loved the Elphbergs well enough, they loved their money more. Thus the King had no resource except in his private possessions, and these were of no great value, saving the Castle and estate of Zenda.

At length, when they had sat late one night and the throws had gone all the evening against the King and for Nikolas, the King flung himself back in the chair, drained his glass, and said impatiently:

"I am weary of the game! Come, my lord, let us end it."

"I would not urge you, sire, a moment beyond what you desire. I play but for your pleasure."

"Then my pleasure has been your profit," said the King with a vexed laugh, "for I believe I am stripped of my last crown. What is my debt?"

The Count, who had the whole sum reckoned on his tablets, took them out, and showed the King the amount of the debt.

"I cannot pay it," said Rudolf. "I would play you again, to double the debt or wipe it out, but I have nothing of value enough to stake."

The desire which had been nursed for long in the Count's heart now saw the moment of its possible realization.

He leaned over the table, and, smoothing his beard with his hand, said gently:

"The amount is no more than half the value of your Majesty's castle and demesne of Zenda."

The King started and forced a laugh.

"Aye, Zenda spoils the prospect from Festenburg, does it?" said he. "But I will not risk Zenda. An Elphberg without Zenda would seem like a man robbed of his wife. We have had it since we have had anything or been anything. I should not seem King without it."

"As you will, sire. Then the debt stands?" He looked full and keenly into the King's eyes, asking without words, "How will you pay it?" and adding without words, "Paid it must be." And the King read the unspoken words in the eyes of Count Nikolas.

The King took up his glass, but finding it empty flung it angrily on the floor, where it shivered into fragments at Count Nikolas's feet; and he shifted in his chair and cursed softly under his breath. Nikolas sat with the dice box in his hand and a smile on his lips; for he knew that the King could not pay, and therefore must play, and he was in the vein, and did not doubt of winning from the King Zenda and its demesne. Then he would be the greatest lord in the kingdom, and hold for his own a kingdom within the kingdom, and the two strongest places in all the land. And a greater prize might then dangle in reach of his grasp.

"The devil spurs and I gallop," said the King at last. And he took up the dice box and rattled it.

"Fortune will smile on you this time, sire, and I shall not grieve at it," said Count Nikolas with a courteous smile.

"Curses on her!" cried the King. "Come, my lord, a quick ending to it! One throw, and I am a free man, or you are master of my castle!"

"One throw let it be, sire, for it grows late," assented Nikolas with a careless air; and they both raised the boxes and rattled the dice inside them. The King threw; his throw was a six and a five, and a sudden gleam of hope lit up his eyes; he leaned forward in his chair, gripping the elbows of it with his hands; his cheeks flushed and his breath came quickly. With a bow Count Nikolas raised his hand and threw. The dice fell and rolled on the table. The King sank back; and the Count said with a smile of apology and a shrug of his shoulders:

"Indeed I am ashamed. For I cannot be denied tonight."

For Count Nikolas of Festenburg had thrown sixes, and thereby won from the King the castle and demesne of Zenda.

He rose from his chair, and, having buckled on his sword that had lain on the table by him, and taken his hat in his hand, stood looking down on the King with a malicious smile on his face. And he said with a look that had more mockery than respect in it:

"Have I your Majesty's leave to withdraw? For ere day dawn, I have matters to transact in Strelsau, and I would be at my castle of Zenda tonight."

The King Rudolf took a sheet of paper and wrote an order that the castle, and all that was in it, and all the demesne should be surrendered to Count Nikolas of Festenburg on his demand, and he gave the paper to Nikolas. Then he rose up and held out his hand, which Nikolas kissed, smiling covertly, and the King said with grace and dignity:

"Cousin, my castle has found a more worthy master. God give you joy of it."

And he motioned with his hand to be left alone. Then, when the Count had gone, he sat down in his chair again, and remained there till it was full day, neither moving nor yet sleeping. There he was found by his gentlemen when they came to dress him, but none asked him what had passed.

Count Nikolas, now Lord of Zenda, did not so waste time, and the matters that he had spoken of did not keep him long in Strelsau; but in the early morning he rode out, the paper which the King had written in his belt.

First he rode with all speed to his own house of Festenburg, and there he gathered together all his followers, servants, foresters, and armed retainers, and he told them that they were to ride with him to Zenda, for that Zenda was now his and not the King's. At this they were greatly astonished, but they ate the fine dinner and drank the wine which he provided, and in the evening they rode down the hill very merry, and trotted, nearly a hundred strong, through the town, making a great noise, so that they disturbed the Bishop of Modenstein, who was lying that night at the inn in the course of a journey from his see to the capital; but nobody could tell the Bishop why they rode to Zenda, and presently the Bishop, being wearied with traveling, went to his bed.

Now King Rudolf, in his chagrin and dismay,

had himself forgotten, or had at least neglected to warn the Count of Festenburg, that his sister Princess Osra was residing at the castle of Zenda; for it was her favorite resort, and she often retired from the court and spent many days there alone. There she was now with two of her ladies, a small retinue of servants, and no more than half-a-dozen guards; and when Count Nikolas came to the gate, it being then after nine, she had gone to her own chamber, and sat before the mirror, dressed in a loose white gown, with her ruddy hair unbound and floating over her shoulders. She was reading an old storybook, containing tales of Helen of Troy, of Cleopatra, of Berenice, and other lovely ladies, very elegantly related and embellished with fine pictures. And the Princess, being very much absorbed in the stories, did not hear nor notice the arrival of the Count's company, but continued to read, while Nikolas roused the watchmen, and the bridge was let down, and the steward summoned. Then Nikolas took the steward aside, and showed him the King's order, bearing the King's seal, and the steward, although both greatly astonished and greatly grieved, could not deny the letter or the seal, but declared himself ready to obey and to surrender the castle; and the sergeant in command of the guard said the same; but, they added, since the Princess was in the castle, they must inform her of the matter, and take her commands.

"Aye, do," said Nikolas, sitting down in the great hall. "Tell her not to be disturbed, but to give me the honor of being her host for as long as she will, and say that I will wait on her, if it be her pleasure."

But he smiled to think of the anger and scorn with which Osra would receive the tidings when the steward delivered them to her.

In this respect the event did not fall short of his expectations, for she was so indignant and aghast that, thinking of nothing but the tidings, she flung away the book and cried: "Send the Count here to me," and stood waiting for him there in her chamber, in her white gown and with her hair unbound and flowing down over her shoulders. And when he came she cried: "What is this, my lord?" and listened to his story with parted lips and flashing eyes, and thus read the King's letter and saw the King's seal. And her eyes filled with tears, but she dashed them away with her hand. Then the Count said, bowing to her as mockingly as he had bowed to her brother:

"It is the fortune of the dice, madame."

"Yes, my lord, as you play the game," said she.

His eyes were fixed on her, and it seemed to him that she was more beautiful in her white gown and with her hair unbound over her shoulders, than he had ever felt her to be before, and he eyed her closely. Suddenly she looked at him, and for a moment she averted his eyes; but he looked again and her eyes met his. For several moments she stood rigid and motionless. Then she said:

"My lord, the King has lost the castle of Zenda, which is the home and cradle of our House. It was scarcely the King's alone to lose. Have I no title in it?"

"It was the King's, madame, and now it is mine," smiled Nikolas.

"Well, then, it is yours," said she, and taking a

135

step towards him, she said: "Have you a mind to venture it again, my lord?"

"I would venture it only against a great stake," said he, smiling still, while his eyes were fixed on her face and marked every change in the color of her cheeks.

"I can play dice as well as the King," she cried. "Are we not all gamblers, we Elphbergs?" And she laughed bitterly.

"But what would your stake be?" he asked sneeringly.

Princess Osra's face was now very pale, but her voice did not tremble and she did not flinch; for the honor of her House and of the throne was as sacred to her as her salvation, and more than her happiness.

"A stake, my lord," said she, "that many gentlemen have thought above any castle in preciousness."

"Of what do you speak?" he asked and his voice quivered a little, as a man's does in excitement. "For, pardon me, madame, but what have you of such value?"

"I have what the poorest girl has, and it is of the value that it pleased God to make it and pleases men to think it," said Osra. "And all of it I will stake against the King's Castle of Zenda and its demesne."

Count Nikolas's eyes flashed and he drew nearer to her; he took his dice box from his pocket, and he held it up before her, and he whispered in an eager hoarse voice:

"Name this great stake, madame; what is it?"

"It is myself, my lord," said Princess Osra.

"Yourself?" he cried wondering, though he had half guessed.

"Aye. To be the Lord of Zenda is much. Is it not more to be husband to the King's sister?"

"It is more," said he, "when the King's sister is the Princess Osra." And he looked at her now with open admiration. But she did not heed his glance, but with face pale as death she seized a small table and drew it between them and cried: "Throw then, my lord! We know the stakes."

"If you win, Zenda is yours. If I win, you are mine."

"Yes, I and Zenda also," said she. "Throw, my lord!"

"Shall we throw thrice, madame, or once, or how often?"

"Thrice, my lord," she answered, tossing back her hair behind her neck, and holding one hand to her side. "Throw first," she added.

The count rattled the box; and the throw was seven. Osra took the box from him, looked keenly and defiantly in his eyes, and threw.

"Fortune is with you, madame," said he, biting his lips. "For a five and a four make nine, or I err greatly."

He took the box from her; his hand shook, but hers was firm and steady; and again he threw.

"Ah, it is but five," said he impatiently, and a frown settled on his brow.

"It is enough, my lord," said Osra, and pointed to the dice that she had thrown, a three and a one.

The Count's eyes gleamed again; he sprang towards her, and was about to seize the box.

But he checked himself suddenly, and bowed, saying:

"Throw first this time, I pray you, madame, if it be not disagreeable to you."

"I do not care which way it is," said Osra, and she shook and made her third cast. When she lifted the box, the face of the dice showed seven. A smile broadened on the Count's lips, for he thought surely he could beat seven, he that had beaten eleven and thereby won the Castle of Zenda, which now he staked against the Princess Osra. But his eyes were very keenly and attentively on her, and he held the box poised, shoulder-high, in his right hand.

Then a sudden faintness and sickness seized on the Princess, and the composure that had hitherto upheld her failed; she could not meet his glance, nor could she bear to see the fall of the dice; but she turned away her head before he threw, and stood thus with averted face. But he kept attentive eyes on her, and drew very near to the table so that he stood right over it. And the Princess Osra caught sight of her own face in the mirror, and started to see herself pallid and ghastly, and her features drawn as though she were suffering some great pain. Yet she uttered no sound.

The dice rattled in the box; they rattled on the table; there was a pause while a man might quickly count a dozen; and then Count Nikolas of Festenburg cried out in a voice that trembled and tripped over the words:

"Eight, eight, eight!"

But before the last of the words had left his shaking lips, the Princess Osra faced round on him like lightning. She raised her hand so that the loose white sleeve fell back from her rounded arm, and her eyes flashed, and her lips curled as she outstretched her arm at him, and cried:

"Foul play!"

For, as she watched her own pale face in the mirror—the mirror which Count Nikolas had not heeded—she had seen him throw, she had seen him stand for an instant over the dice he had thrown with gloomy and maddened face; and then she had seen a slight swift movement of his left hand, as his fingers deftly darted down and touched one of the dice and turned it. And all this she had seen before he had cried eight. Therefore now she turned on him, and cried, "Foul play!" and before he could speak, she darted by him towards the door. But he sprang forward, and caught her by the arm above the wrist and gripped her, and his fingers bit into the flesh of her arm, as he gasped, "You lie! Where are you going?" But her voice rang out clear and loud in answer:

"I am going to tell all the world that Zenda is ours again, and I am going to publish in every city in the kingdom that Count Nikolas of Festenburg is a common cheat and rogue, and should be whipped at the cart's tail through the streets of Strelsau. For I saw you in the mirror, my lord, I saw you in the mirror!" And she ended with a wild laugh that echoed through the room.

Still he gripped her arm, and she did not flinch; for an instant he looked full in her eyes; covetousness, and desire, and shame, came all together upon him, and overmastered him, and he hissed between set teeth:

"You shan't! By God, you shan't!"

"Aye, but I will, my lord," said Osra. "It is a fine tale for the King and for your friends in Strelsau."

An instant longer he held her where she was; and he gasped and licked his lips. Then he suddenly dragged her with him towards a couch; seizing up a coverlet that lay on the couch he flung it round her, and he folded it tight about her, and he drew it close over her face. She could not cry out nor move. He lifted her up and swung her over his shoulder, and, opening the door of the room, dashed down the stairs towards the great hall.

In the great hall were six of the King's Guard, and some of the servants of the castle, and many of the people who had come with Count Nikolas; they all sprang to their feet when they saw him. He took no heed of them, but rushed at a run through the hall, and out under the portcullis and across the bridge, which had not been raised since he entered. There at the end of the bridge a lackey held his horse; and he leaped on his horse, setting one hand on the saddle, and still holding Osra; and then he cried aloud:

"My men follow me! To Festenburg!"

And all his men ran out, the King's Guard doing nothing to hinder them, and jumping on their horses and setting them at a gallop, hurried after the Count. He, riding furiously, turned towards the town of Zenda, and the whole company swept down the hill, and, reaching the town, clattered and dashed through it at full gallop, neither drawing rein nor turning to right or left; and again they roused the Bishop of Modenstein, and he turned in his bed, wondering what the rush of mounted men meant. But they, galloping still, climbed the opposite hill and came to the castle of Festenburg with their horses spent and foundered. In they all crowded, close on one another's heels; the bridge was drawn up; and there in the entrance they stood looking at one another, asking mutely what their master had done, and who was the lady whom he carried wrapped in the coverlet. But he ran on till he reached the stairs, and he climbed them, and entering a room in the gate tower, looking over the moat, he laid the Princess Osra on a couch, and standing over her he smote one hand upon the other, and he swore loudly:

"Now, as God lives, Zenda I will have, and her I will have, and it shall be her husband whom she must, if she will, proclaim a cheat in Strelsau!"

Then he bent down and lifted the coverlet from her face. But she did not stir nor speak, nor open her eyes. For she had fallen into a swoon as they rode, and did not know what had befallen her, nor where she had been brought, nor that she was now in the Castle of Festenburg, and in the power of a desperate man. Thus she lay still and white, while Count Nikolas stood over her and bit his nails in rage. And it was then just on midnight.

On being disturbed for the third time, the Bishop of Modenstein, whose temper was hot and cost him continual prayers and penances from the mastery it strove to win over him, was very impatient; and since he was at once angry and half asleep, it was long before he could or would understand the monstrous news with which his terrified host came trembling and quaking to his bedside in the dead of the night. A servant girl, stammered the frightened fellow, had run down half dressed and panting from the castle of Zenda, and declared that whether they chose to believe her or not—and, indeed, she could hardly believe such a thing herself, although she had seen it with her own eyes from her own window—yet Count Nikolas of Festenburg had come to the castle that evening, had spoken with Princess Osra, and now (they might call her a liar if they chose) had carried off the Princess with him on his horse to Festenburg, alive or dead none knew; and the menservants were amazed and terrified, and the soldiers were at their wits' end, talking big and threatening to bring ten thousand men from Strelsau and to leave not one stone upon another at Festenburg, and what not. But all the while and for all their big talk nothing was done; and the Princess was at Festenburg, alive or dead or in what strait none knew. And, finally, nobody but one poor servant girl had had the wit to run down and rouse the town.

The Bishop of Modenstein sat up in his bed and he fairly roared at the innkeeper:

"Are there no men, then, who can fight in the town, fool?"

"None, none, my lord—not against the Count. Count Nikolas is a terrible man. Please God, he has not killed the Princess by now."

"Saddle my horse," said the Bishop, "and be quick with it."

And he leaped out of bed with sparkling eyes.

For the Bishop was a young man, but a little turned of thirty, and he was a noble of the old house of Hentzau. Now some of the Hentzaus (of whom history tells us of many) have been good, and some have been bad; and the good fear God, while the bad do not; but neither the good nor the bad fear anything in the world besides. Hence, for good or ill, they do great deeds and risk their lives as another man risks a penny. So the Bishop, leaving his bed, dressed himself in breeches and boots, and set a black hat with a violet feather on his head, and, staying to put on nothing else but his shirt and his cloak over it, in ten minutes was on his horse at the door of the inn. For a moment he looked at a straggling crowd that had gathered there; then with a toss of his head and a curl of his lip he told them what he thought of them, saying openly that he thanked heaven they were not of his diocese, and in an instant he was galloping through the streets of the town towards the Castle of Festenburg, with his sword by his side, and a brace of pistols in the holsters of the saddles. Thus he left the gossipers and vaporers behind, and rode alone as he was up the hill, his blood leaping and his heart beating quick; for, as he went, he said to himself:

"It is not often a Churchman has a chance like this."

On the stroke of half-past twelve he came to the bridge of the castle moat, and the bridge was up. But the Bishop shouted, and the watchman came out and stood in the gateway across the moat, and, the night being fine and clear, he presented an excellent aim.

"My pistol is straight at your head," cried the Bishop. "Let down the bridge. I am Frederick of Hentzau; that is, I am the Bishop of Modenstein, and I charge you, if you are a dutiful son of the Church, to obey me. The pistol is full at your head."

The watchman knew the Bishop, but he also knew the Count his master.

"I dare not let down the bridge without an order from my lord," he faltered.

"Then before you can turn round, you're a dead man," said the Bishop.

"Will you hold me harmless with my lord, if I let it down?"

"Aye, he shall not hurt you. But if you do not immediately let it down, I'll shoot you first and refuse you Christian burial afterwards. Come, down with it."

So the watchman, fearing that, if he refused, the Bishop would spare neither body nor soul, but would destroy the one and damn the other, let down the bridge, and the Bishop, leaping from his horse, ran across with his drawn sword in one hand and a pistol in the other. Walking into the hall, he found a great company of Count Nikolas's men, drinking with one another, but talking uneasily and seeming alarmed. And the Bishop raised the hand that held the sword above his head in the attitude of benediction, saying, "Peace be with you!"

Most of them knew him by his face, and all knew him as soon as a comrade whispered his name, and they sprang to their feet, uncovering their heads and bowing. And he said:

"Where is your master the Count?"

"The Count is upstairs, my lord," they answered. "You cannot see him now."

"Nay, but I will see him," said the Bishop.

"We are ordered to let none pass," said they, and although their manner was full of respect, they spread themselves across the hall, and thus barred the way to the staircase that rose in the corner of the hall. But the Bishop faced them in great anger, crying:

"Do you think I do not know what has been done? Are you all, then, parties in this treachery? Do you all want to swing from the turrets of the castle when the King comes with a thousand men from Strelsau?"

At this they looked at him and at one another with great uneasiness; for they knew that the King had no mercy when he was roused, and that he loved his sister above everybody in the world. And the Bishop stepped up close to their rank. Then one of them drew his sword halfway from its scabbard. But the Bishop, perceiving this, cried:

"Do you all do violence to a lady, and dare to lay hands on the King's sister? Aye, and here is a fellow that would strike a Bishop of God's Church!" And he caught the fellow a buffet with the flat of his sword, that knocked him down. "Let me pass, you rogues," said the Bishop. "Do you think you can stop a Hentzau?"

"Let us go and tell the Count that my lord the Bishop is here," cried the house steward, thinking that he had found a way out of the difficulty; for they dared neither to touch the Bishop nor yet to let him through; and the steward turned to run towards the staircase. But the Bishop sprang after him, quick as an arrow, and, dropping the pistol from his left hand, caught him by the shoulder and hurled him back. "I want no announcing," he said. "The Church is free to enter everywhere." And he burst through them at the point of the sword, reckless now what might befall him so that he made his way through. But they did not venture to cut him down; for they knew that nothing but death would stop him, and for their very souls' sake they dared not kill him. So he, kicking one and pushing another and laying about him with the flat of his sword and with his free hand, and reminding them all the while of their duty to the Church and of his sacred character, at last made his way through and stood alone, unhurt, at the foot of the staircase, while they cowered by the walls or looked at him in stupid helplessness and bewilderment. And the Bishop swiftly mounted the stairs.

At this instant in the room in the gate tower of the castle overlooking the moat there had fallen a moment of dead silence. Here Count Nikolas had raised the Princess, set her on a couch, and waited till her faintness and fright were gone. Then he had come near to her, and in brief harsh tones told her his mind. For him, indeed, the dice were now cast; in his fury and fear he had dared all. He was calm now, with the calmness of a man at a great turn of fate. That room, he told her, she should never leave alive, save as his promised wife, sworn and held to secrecy and silence by the force of that bond and of her oath. If he killed her he must die, whether by his own hand or the King's mattered little. But he would die for a great cause and in a great venture. "I shall not be called a cheating gamester, madame," said he, a smile on his pale face. "I choose death sooner than disgrace. Such is my choice. What is yours? It stands between death and silence; and no man but your husband will dare to trust your silence."

"You do not dare to kill me," said she defiantly.

"Madame, I dare do nothing else. They may write 'murderer' on my tomb; they shall not throw 'cheat' in my living face."

"I will not be silent," cried Osra, springing to her feet. "And rather than be your wife I would die a thousand times. For a cheat you are—a cheat—a cheat!" Her voice rose, till he feared that she would be heard, if anyone chanced to listen, even from so far off as the hall. Yet he made one more effort, seeking to move her by an appeal to which women are not wont to be insensible.

"A cheat, yes!" said he. "I, Nikolas of Festenburg, am a cheat. I say it, though no other man shall while I live to hear him. But to gain what stake?"

"Why, my brother's Castle of Zenda."

"I swear to you it was not," he cried, coming nearer to her. "I did not fear losing on the cast, but I could not endure not to win. Not my stake, madame, but yours lured me to my foul play. Have you your face, and yet do not know to what it drives men?"

147

"If I have a fair face, it should inspire fair deeds," said she. "Do not touch me, sir, do not touch me. I loathe breathing the same air with you, or so much as seeing your face. Aye, and I can die. Even the women of our House know how to die."

At her scorn and contempt a great rage came upon him, and he gripped the hilt of his sword, and drew it from the scabbard. But she stood still, facing him with calm eyes. Her lips moved for a moment in prayer, but she did not shrink.

"I pray you," said he in trembling speech, mastering himself for an instant. "I pray you!" But he could say no more.

"I will cry your cheating in all Strelsau," said she.

"Then commend your soul to God. For in one minute you shall die."

Still she stood motionless; and he began to come near to her, his sword now drawn in his hand. Having come within the distance from which he could strike her, he paused and gazed into her eyes. She answered him with a smile. Then there was for an instant the utter stillness in the room; and in that instant the Bishop of Modenstein set his foot on the staircase and came running up. On a sudden Osra heard the step, and a gleam flashed in her eye. The Count heard it also, and his sword was arrested in its stroke. A smile came on his face. He was glad at the coming of someone whom he might kill in fight; for it turned him sick to butcher her unresisting. Yet he dared not let her go, to cry his cheating in the streets of Strelsau. The steps came nearer.

He dropped his sword on the floor and sprang upon her. A shriek rang out, but he pressed his hand on her mouth and seized her in his arms. She had not strength to resist, and he carried her swiftly across the room to a door in the wall. He pulled the door open—it was very heavy and massive—and he flung her down roughly on the stone floor of a little chamber, square and lofty, having but one small window high up, through which the moonlight scarcely pierced. She fell with a moan of pain. Unheeding, he turned on his heel and shut the door. And, as he turned, he heard a man throw himself against the door of the room. It also was strong, and twice the man hurled himself with all his force against it. At last it strained and gave way; and the Bishop of Modenstein burst into the room breathless. And he saw no trace of the Princess's presence, but only Count Nikolas standing sword in hand in front of the door in the wall with a sneering smile on his face.

The Bishop of Modenstein never loved to speak afterwards of what followed, saying always that he rather deplored than gloried in it, and that when a man of sacred profession was forced to use the weapons of this world it was a matter of grief to him, not of vaunting. But the King compelled him by urgent requests to describe the whole affair, while the Princess was never weary of telling all that she knew, or of blessing all bishops for the sake of the Bishop of Modenstein. Yet the Bishop blamed himself; perhaps, if the truth were known, not for the necessity that drove him to do what he did, as much as for a secret and ashamed joy which he detected in himself. For certainly, as he burst into the room now, there was no sign of reluctance or unwillingness in his face; he took off his feathered hat, bowed politely to the Count, and resting the point of his sword on the floor asked:

"My lord, where is the Princess?"

"What do you want here, and who are you?" cried the Count with a blasphemous oath.

"When we were boys together, you knew Frederick of Hentzau. Do you not now know the Bishop of Modenstein?"

"Bishop! This is no place for bishops. Get back to your prayers, my lord."

"It wants some time yet before matins," answered the Bishop. "My lord, where is the Princess?"

"What do you want with her?"

"I am here to escort her wherever it may be her pleasure to go."

He spoke confidently, but he was in his heart alarmed and uneasy because he had not found the Princess.

"I do not know where she is," said Nikolas of Festenburg.

"My lord, you lie," said the Bishop of Modenstein.

The Count had wanted nothing but an excuse for attacking the intruder. He had it now, and an angry flush mounted in his cheeks as he walked across to where the Bishop stood.

Shifting his sword, which he had picked up again, to his left hand, he struck the Bishop on the face with his gloved hand. The Bishop smiled and turned the other cheek to Count Nikolas, who struck him again with all his force, so that he reeled back, catching hold of the open door to avoid falling, and the blood started dull red under the skin of his face. But he still smiled, and bowed, saying:

"I find nothing about the third blow in Holy Scripture."

At this instant the Princess Osra, who had been half stunned by the violence with which Nikolas had thrown her on the floor, came to her full sense, and, hearing the Bishop's voice, she cried out loudly for help. He, hearing her, darted in an instant across the room, and was at the door of the little chamber before the Count could stop him. He pulled the door open and Osra sprang out to him, saying:

"Save me! Save me!"

"You are safe, madame, have no fear," answered the Bishop. And turning to the Count, he continued: "Let us go outside, my lord, and discuss this matter. Our dispute will disturb and perhaps alarm the Princess."

And a man might have read the purpose in his eyes, though his manner and words were gentle; for he had sworn in his heart that the Count should not escape.

But the Count cared as little for the presence of the Princess as he had for her dignity, her honor, or her life: and now that she was no longer wholly at his mercy, but there was a new chance that she might escape, his rage and the fear of exposure lashed him to fury, and, without more talking, he made at the Bishop, crying:

"You first, and then her! I'll be rid of the pair of you!"

The Bishop faced him, standing between Princess Osra and his assault, while she shrank back a little, sheltering herself behind the heavy door. For although she had been ready to die without fear, yet the sight of men fighting frightened her, and she veiled her face with her hands, and waited in dread to hear the sound of their swords clashing. But the Bishop looked very happy, and, setting his hat on his head with a jaunty air, he stood on guard. For ten years or more he had not used his sword, but the secret of its mastery seemed to revive, fresh and clear in his mind, and let his soul say what it would, his body rejoiced to be at the exercise again, so that his blood kindled and his eyes gleamed in the glee of strife. Thus he stepped forward, guarding himself, and thus he met the Count's impetuous onset; he neither flinched nor gave back, but finding himself holding his own, he pressed on and on, not violently attacking and yet never resting, and turning every thrust with a wrist of iron. And while Osra now gazed with wide eyes and close-held breath and Count Nikolas muttered oaths and grew more furious, the Bishop seemed as gay as when he talked to the King more gaily, maybe, than Bishops should. Again his eye danced as in the days when he had been called the wildest of the Hentzaus. And still he drove Count Nikolas back and back.

Now behind the Count was a window, which he himself had caused to be enlarged and made low and wide, in order that he might look from it over the surrounding country; in time of war it was covered with a close and strong iron grating. But now the grating was off and the window open, and beneath the window was a fall of fifty feet or hard upon it into the moat below. The Count, looking into the Bishop's face and seeing him smile, suddenly recollected the window, and fancied it was the Bishop's design to drive him on it so that he could give back no more; and since he knew by now that the Bishop was his master with the sword, a despairing rage settled upon him; determining to die swiftly, since die he must, he rushed forward, making a desperate lunge at his enemy. But the Bishop parried the lunge, and, always seeming to be about to run the Count through the body, again forced him to retreat till his back was close to the opening of the window. Here Nikolas stood, his eyes glaring like a madman's; then a sudden devilish smile spread over his face.

"Will you yield yourself, my lord?" cried the Bishop, putting a restraint on the wicked impulse to kill the man, and lowering his point for an instant.

In that short moment the Count made his last throw; for all at once, as it seemed, and almost in one motion, he thrust and wounded the Bishop in the left side of his body, high in the chest near the shoulder, and, though the wound was slight, the blood flowed freely; then drawing back his sword, he seized it by the blade halfway up and flung it like a javelin at the Princess, who stood still by the door, breathlessly watching the fight. By an ace it missed her head, and it pinned a tress of her hair to the door and quivered deep-set in the wood of the door. When the Bishop of Modenstein saw this, hesitation and mercy passed out of his heart, and though the man had now no weapon, he thought of sparing him no more than he would have spared any cruel and savage beast, but he drove his sword into his body, and the Count, not being able to endure the thrust without flinching, against his own will gave back before it. Then came from his lips a loud cry of dismay and despair; for at the same moment that the sword was in him he, staggering back, fell wounded to death through the open window. The Bishop looked out after him, and Princess Osra heard the sound of a great splash in the water of the moat below; for very horror she sank against the door, seeming to be held up more by the sword that had pinned her hair than by her own strength. Then came up through the window, from which the Bishop still looked with a strange smile, the clatter of a hundred feet, running to the gate of the castle. The bridge was let down; the confused sound of many men talking, of whispers, of shouts, and of cries of horror, mounted up through the air. For the Count's men in the hall also had heard the splash, and run out to see what it was, and there they beheld the body of their master, dead in the moat; their eyes were wide open, and they could hardly lay their tongues to the words as they pointed to the body and whispered to one another, very low: "The Bishop has killed him—the Bishop has killed him." But the Bishop saw them from the window, and leaned out, crying:

"Yes, I have killed him. So perish all such villains!"

When they looked up, and saw in the moonlight the Bishop's face, they were amazed. But he hastily drew his head in, so that they might not see him anymore. For he knew that his face had been fierce, and exultant, and joyful. Then, dropping his sword, he ran across to the Princess; he drew the Count's sword, which was wet with his own blood, out of the door, releasing the Princess's hair; and, seeing that she was very faint, he put his arm about her, and led her to the couch; she sank upon it, trembling and white as her white gown, and murmuring: "Fearful, fearful!" and she clutched his arm, and for a long while she would not let him go; and her eyes were fixed on the Count's sword that lay on the floor by the entrance of the little room.

"Courage, madame," said the Bishop softly. "All danger is past. The villain is dead, and you are with the most devoted of your servants."

"Yes, yes," she said, and pressed his arm and shivered. "Is he really dead?"

"He is dead. God have mercy on him," said the Bishop.

"And you killed him?"

"I killed him. If it were a sin, pray God forgive me!"

Up through the window still came the noise of voices and the stir of men moving; for they were recovering the body of the Count from the moat; yet neither Osra nor the Bishop noticed any longer what was passing; he was intent on her, and she seemed hardly yet herself; but suddenly,

before he could interpose, she threw herself off the
couch and onto her knees in front of him, and,
seizing hold of his hand, she kissed first the
episcopal ring that he wore and then his hand. For
he was both Bishop and a gallant gentleman, and a
kiss she gave him for each; and after she had kissed
his hand, she held it in both of hers as though for
safety's sake she clung to it. But he raised her
hastily, crying to her not to kneel before him, and,
throwing away his hat, he knelt before her, kissing
her hands many times. She seemed now recovered
from her bewilderment and terror; for as she
looked down on him kneeling, she was halfway
between tears and smiles, and with curving lips
but wet shining eyes she said very softly:

"Ah, my lord, who made a bishop of you?"
And her cheeks grew in an instant from dead white
into suddenly red, and her hand moved over his
head as if she would fain have touched him with it.
And she bent down ever so little towards him. Yet,
perhaps, it was nothing; any lady, who had seen
how he bore himself, and knew that it was in her
cause, for her honor and life, might well have done
the same.

The Bishop of Modenstein made no immediate
answer; his head was still bowed over her hand, and
after a while he kissed her hand again; and he felt
her hand press his. Then suddenly, as though in
alarm, she drew her hand away, and he let it go
easily. Then he raised his eyes and met the glance of
hers, and he smiled; and Osra also smiled. For an
instant they were thus. Then the Bishop rose to his
feet, and he stood before her with bent head and
eyes that sought the ground in becoming humility.

"It is by God's infinite goodness and divine permission that I hold my sacred office," said he. "I would that I were more worthy of it! But today I have taken pleasure in the killing of a man."

"And in the saving of a lady, sir," she added softly, "who will ever count you among her dearest friends and the most gallant of her defenders. Is God angry at such a deed as that?"

"May He forgive us all our sins," said the Bishop gravely; but what other sins he had in his mind he did not say, nor did the Princess ask him.

Then he gave her his arm, and they two walked together down the stairs into the hall; the Bishop, having forgotten both his hat and his sword, was bareheaded and had no weapon in his hand. The Count's men were all collected in the hall, being crowded round a table that stood by the wall; for on the table lay the body of Count Nikolas of Festenburg, and it was covered with a horse cloth that one of the servants had thrown over it. But when the men saw the Princess and the Bishop, they made way for them and stood aside, bowing low as they passed.

"You bow now," said Osra, "but, before, none of you would lift a finger for me. To my lord the Bishop alone do I owe my life; and he is a Churchman, while you were free to fight for me. For my part, I do not envy your wives such husbands"; and with a most scornful air she passed between their ranks, taking great and ostentatious care not to touch one of them even with the hem of her gown. At this they grew red and shuffled on their feet; and one or two swore under their breath; and thanked God their wives were not such shrews, being indeed very much ashamed of themselves, and very uneasy at thinking what these same wives of theirs would say to them when the thing came to be known. But Osra and the Bishop passed over the bridge, and he set her on his horse. The summer morning had just dawned, clear and fair, so that the sun caught her ruddy hair as she mounted in her white gown. But the Bishop took the bridle of the horse and led it at a foot's pace down the hill and into the town.

Now by this time the news of what had chanced had run all through the town, and the people were out in the streets, gossiping and guessing. And when they saw the Princess Osra safe and sound and smiling, and the Bishop in his shirt—for he had given his cloak to her—leading the horse, they broke into great cheering. The men cheered the Princess, while the women thrust themselves to the front rank of the crowd, and blessed the Bishop of Modenstein. But he walked with his head down and his eyes on the ground, and would not look up, even when the women cried out in great fear and admiration on seeing that his shirt was stained with his blood and with the blood of Nikolas of Festenburg that had spurted out upon it. But one thing the Princess heard, which sent her cheeks red again: for a buxom girl glanced merrily at her, and made bold to say in a tone that the Princess could not but hear:

"By the Saints, here's waste! If he were not a churchman, now!" And her laughing eye traveled from the Princess to him, and back to the Princess again.

158

"Shall we go a little faster?" whispered Osra, bending down to the Bishop. But the girl only thought that she whispered something else, and laughed the more.

At last they passed the town, and with a great crowd still following them came to the castle. At the gate of it the Bishop stopped, and aided the Princess to alight. Again he knelt and kissed her hand, saying only:

"Madame, farewell!"

"Farewell, my lord," said Osra softly; and she went hastily into the castle, while the Bishop returned to his inn in the town, and though the people stood round the inn the best part of the day, calling and watching for him, he would not show himself.

In the evening of that day the King, having heard the tidings of the crime of Count Nikolas, came in furious haste with a troop of horse from Strelsau. And when he heard how Osra had played at dice with the Count, and staking herself against the castle of Zenda had won it back, he was ashamed, and swore an oath that he would play dice no more, which oath he faithfully observed. But in the morning of the next day he went to Festenburg, where he flogged soundly every man who had not run away before his coming; and all the possessions of Count Nikolas he confiscated, and he pulled down the Castle of Festenburg, and filled up the moat that had run round its walls.

Then he sent for the Bishop of Modenstein, and thanked him, offering to him all the demesne of Count Nikolas; but the Bishop would not accept it, nor any mark of the King's favor, not even the Order of the Red Rose. Therefore the King granted the ground on which the castle stood, and all the lands belonging to it, to Francis of Tarlenheim, brother-in-law to the wife of Prince Henry, who built the chateau which now stands there and belongs to the same family to this day.

But the Bishop of Modenstein, having been entertained by the King with great splendor for two days, would not stay longer, but set out to pursue his journey, clad now in his ecclesiastical garments. And Princess Osra sat by her window, leaning her head on her hand, and watching him till the trees of the forest hid him; and once, when he was on the edge of the forest, he turned his face for an instant, and looked back at her where she sat watching in the window. Thus he went to Strelsau; and when he was come there, he sent immediately for his confessor, and the confessor, having heard him, laid upon him a severe penance, which he performed with great zeal, exactness, and contrition. But whether the penance was for killing Count Nikolas of Festen-burg (which in a layman, at least, would have seemed but a venial sin) or for what else, who shall say?

About the authors:

Rudyard Kipling *was born in India in 1865 to British parents. World-famous for such books as* Just So Stories, The Jungle Books, *and* Kim, *Kipling was awarded the Nobel prize for literature in 1907.*

Robert Louis Stevenson *was born in Scotland. Though he studied engineering and law, he decided instead to become a writer. Three of his most famous novels are* Kidnapped, Treasure Island, *and* The Strange Case of Dr. Jekyll and Mr. Hyde.

Arthur Conan Doyle *is best known as the creator of Sherlock Holmes, perhaps the world's most famous detective. Doyle was knighted in 1902.*

Stanley Weyman, *born in 1855, practiced law for eight years before turning to writing. He is the author of many historical adventure stories.*

Anthony Hope, *the pen name of Sir Anthony Hope Hawkins, was born in England in 1863. He is best known for his thrilling adventure story,* The Prisoner of Zenda.